SWEET & CRAZY

SWEET & CRAZY

PATTY DANN

ST. MARTIN'S GRIFFIN ✠ NEW YORK

www.stmartins.com

Library of Congress Cataloing-in-Publication Data

Dann, Patty.
    Sweet & crazy / Patty Dann.
      p. cm.
    title: Sweet and crazy
    ISBN 0-312-31666-6 (hc)
    ISBN 0-312-31667-4 (pbk)
    EAN 978-0312-31667-9
    1. Windows—Fiction. 2. Racism—Fiction. 3. Single mothers—Fiction 4. Mothers and sons—Fiction. 5. September 11 Terrorist Attacks, 2001—Fiction. 6. Ohio—Fiction. I. Title: Sweet and crazy. II. Title.

PS3554.A575S94   2003
813'.54—dc21

2003047202

First St. Martin's Griffin Edition: November 2004

10 9 8 7 6 5 4 3 2 1

To R. S.

When astronauts landed on the moon in 1969, they carried with them a small piece of fabric from the fragile wing of the plane the Wright brothers flew at Kitty Hawk in 1903.

AUGUST 2001

The cricket-hot night my husband died, my four-year-old-son, Pete, looked at me and said, "Now you're a window," and I did not correct the child. I was thirty-nine years old and worked at the local YMCA, which meant I gave workshops on how to record your life story. Pete said I taught "scribble-scrabble." My students were butchers and bakers and confused people. I also worked in the library at the community college where Ed taught world history. The night Ed died, I stayed up weeping and ironing his shirts.

We lived in a little yellow house in Ash Creek, Ohio. Ash Creek is not a suburb of anywhere. It's a mostly white town, but the two gas stations and cleaners and pizza place were owned by Indians from India. There's an air force base not too far away. I'm a homing pigeon. I grew up in Ash Creek, went one hundred miles west to college, and I came back.

. . .

I'm not quite sure what to do with this widow thing. Some people turn away when they see us on the street, and others give Pete and me a look that makes me feel like we're supposed to be inside with the shades down.

Last night Pete lay in bed, kicking his sheep-and-donkey sheets off him, and said, "Why don't you get to be a baby twice?" I lay next to him for a while after he fell asleep. Then I got up and threw a pair of my husband's old shoes in the garbage.

This morning when Pete saw the shoes in the garbage, he pulled them out, brushed off the eggshells, and said, "Don't you ever throw anything away of Daddy's ever." He dragged a chair to Ed's closet and yanked down all of Ed's shirts, then hauled them to his own closet and hung them on the pole next to his little shirts on little hangers.

One of my students confided to me, "I stopped lying when I turned seventy." I feel like I'm seventy. My aunt Barbara says loss doesn't make you stronger like they tell you in books. She says loss makes you weaker. I wouldn't say that, just that when I walk down the street, I'm stunned there are so many people who are alive.

Ed died at five-thirty in the afternoon. Pete and I were sitting on the couch watching a Blue's Clues video from the library. The tape was a little wobbly. I got up to adjust the tracking, and then I went in to check on Ed. He lay there still as a board in his hospital bed. I ran in to get Pete. "Daddy is going to stop breathing soon," I said.

"How do you know?" said Pete.

"Come here." I held out my hand.

"Don't rewind it," said Pete, pointing to the video.

We went into the room holding hands, and Pete climbed onto his father's bed. He climbed up on Ed and kissed his face. I held Ed's hand, and he stopped breathing.

"He stopped breathing," I whispered.

Pete didn't look at me. He just kept kissing Ed's face and said solemnly, "I guess you won't be having any more birthday parties."

I called the funeral home, and they said, "We can be right over, ma'am."

"No, please," I said. Now a thunderstorm was crashing outside. "No, please give us two hours."

I cannot account exactly for those two hours. There was a time in the Middle Ages when the king decided to change the calendar and people marched around with signs that said, "Give us back our twelve days." I had the sense that someone had altered time like that in those two hours. I do know that Pete kept doing cartwheels, over and over.

Two men in suits and hats, who appeared to be from the 1950s, showed up, shaking rain off themselves. Pete kept saying to them, "How are you going to fit Daddy out the door?" but they did not respond.

We have a narrow front door and back door, and the hallway hooks around so that we had to return a refrigerator we'd ordered, because it was too big.

They told us to leave the room while they wrapped him up, and then they put him on what looked like a hospital gurney and wheeled him out. They tipped him up around the corner. They managed. Pete and I stood out in the pouring rain as the men in suits placed Ed in the back of a black van.

Our neighbor Thomas came out and stood on his porch with a coffee cup in his hand. He has prematurely white hair and blue eyes and was wearing muslin clothes because he works as a cooper at Hill House, the eighteenth-century colonial restoration outside of town. When Ed was fading, Thomas used to leave things on our porch. Once he left a wooden bowl he'd made full of fresh strawberries. Another time he left a small burlap bag of a colonial pancake mix. Unfortunately one of the dogs from down the street chewed on the pancake mix in the night.

After the men from the funeral home left, I picked up Pete and carried him back inside. He was a big kid, but there he was in my arms, like a baby. I made peanut butter sandwiches, and we watched the rest of the Blue's Clues video.

"Now we're two," said Pete.

"What?"

"Now we're two people," he said.

•   •   •

I'm Jewish, which means that for two thousand years my family always married Jews, until I married Ed, who was the son of a Mennonite minister. It does not mean that I'm religious. One year I did make a messily braided challah bread for the annual bake sale at the library. Although I heard several people walk by it displayed on the table filled with Rice Krispies treats and pumpkin bread and say, "Isn't that interesting," I ended up taking it home for Ed and myself at the end of the day. It means that every so often when I look out the front window, I imagine I'm Anne Frank, but it doesn't mean I know Hebrew or am opposed to Christmas trees. In my case, it means I have olive skin and big breasts, even though I'm only a little over five feet tall.

My father died soon after Pete was born. He was a pharmacist in town and my mother was a homemaker. Every time my father met someone new he'd say, "My bride's so neat. When I get up in the middle of the night to go to the bathroom, she makes the bed." He always called her his bride. She died ten months later, the day after Pete began to walk.

People kept bringing food after Ed's funeral. Casseroles were stacked on top of the refrigerator. It looked like I was going to have a Tupperware party. Each night I stood at the sink wolfing down different desserts: a cheesecake, a cherry pie, gooey chocolate chip cookies. And when I couldn't stand it anymore, I threw platefuls out the back door for the birds and the raccoons.

Pete said, "When will everything be regular?"

Last night a telemarketer called and Pete answered the phone, "ThisisPetewhoisthisplease?" he says in one breath. I believe it was a telemarketer, because he replied, "No, he died."

When we knew Ed was going to die, we went to the cemetery and checked it out. We left Pete with a sitter for the afternoon. The man who showed us around held a transistor radio to his ear and was listening to a Reds game as he showed us around.

"Do you want a two-plot or a four-plot, or a six-pack?"

I grabbed Ed's hand tightly and said, "We'll just get a double for now."

"Now, do you want to be buried foot to foot or head to head?"

That afternoon we went to a coffee shop and ordered cheeseburgers for both of us, shared a chocolate milk shake, then went home and made love before I went to pick up Pete.

I've been doing widow research at the library. In India, Hindu women really are supposed to "manifest inconsolable grief for the rest of their lives" after their husbands die. In Swaziland, widows wear a heavy saddle of twisted grass. Here, people came to the door with pesto sauce and gift certificates for massages, but sometimes I feel like I'm wearing a heavy saddle of twisted grass.

In a town in Ireland, widows wear black for one year and then lavender for another after their husbands die. That might solve my clothes dilemma, because I have never quite gotten the hang of it. I would like a uniform of some kind, although lavender might make me look washed out.

Pete got into bed with me this morning and said, "I want to be a veterinarian. We could keep the animals in my room in baskets. But mainly I want a pig."

"A pig."

"I want a real pig to pick me up from school."

"But he couldn't carry your lunch box the way I do while you play on the playground."

"He could just hook it on his ear," said Pete solemnly.

My neighbor Thomas was out on his porch this morning, with his coffee cup, when I stepped out to get the newspaper. He was wearing jeans and a white T-shirt. His white hair was rumpled. I was in my very chic blue-and-white cotton robe with birds on it. I suddenly felt shy, without a bra, and my breasts sagging. But my point is, he didn't say, "How are you doing?"

He said, "Looks like the raccoons are at the garbage again."

"Yes," I said.

And then I went back in. I don't know if he's the least sensitive man in the world or just trying to be normal. If he had said, "How are you doing?" I would have been annoyed, but this raccoon conversation didn't thrill me, either.

My friend Joya, who has two kids and an ex-husband, said, "Hanna, this is a difficult year. Accept it. Everything you do will feel strange. It's a strange time."

I stood in the house behind the closed front door, with our cat, Mimo, crawling around on my feet, and I felt like I'd been on a first date. I think I should put a bra on when I go outside for the paper, or get dressed. That's a better idea, get dressed.

Pete got out of bed and lay down at my feet behind the door. "I wish Ringo was here right now. Are there Beatles in every state?" he said.

This evening, while Pete was watching *Rugrats*, a show that makes me agitated under normal circumstances, a pollster called. "Ma'am, I'm not soliciting for anything. I just want to ask you three questions. "Which is most important to you, health care, gun control, or the environment?"

"Well," I snapped, "my husband just died of brain cancer, so I'm very concerned about health care, and who knows, the environment could have caused it, and I have a small child, so I don't want handguns around. They're all important. I can't choose just one."

"Sorry to have bothered you, ma'am."

I don't like to leave Pete alone too much, but I needed air, so I walked out onto the front porch.

Who should be there, on our porch, but my neighbor Thomas, just standing there on our porch, looking sideways at his house.

My husband never liked Thomas. Mennonites are not supposed to judge anybody. At least that was what I learned when Ed first brought me home. He grew up in a very spare house in Ohio. His father wore tails when he preached. His mother wore an apron every day when he was a child. His father never said, "How could you marry a Jewish girl?"

At that meeting, his father said, "Do you want to hear a Mennonite joke? What do Mennonites like to eat? Soup, soup, and more soup."

Ed's distrust of Thomas started because once when we were away overnight, visiting his father in fact, we returned home and Ed insisted Thomas had taken our local newspaper, *The Ash Creek Falcon*, which was supposed to arrive in our driveway seven days a week. But when we returned that Sunday morning, it was gone. Ed called the service and reported it like it was a felony. It turned out that it had not been delivered, but Ed could not get it out of his head that it was Thomas. Ed took scissors on our honeymoon for clipping articles. That's how serious he was about his newspapers.

Ed leaned back in his chair at the kitchen table the morning after he had called the newspaper service and said, "I'm not sure about our neighbor. I think he covets you."

This was before we knew he had cancer. Looking back, it was an odd thing to say, although now Thomas is out there on my porch, which only a few weeks ago belonged to my husband and me. Either Ed was clairvoyant, or his mind had already begun to addle. As Joya says, "Marriages are as fragile as an egg-and-spoon race."

Thomas, still staring at his own house, said, "You know, in colonial times, ships carrying bags of rice were a dangerous thing. If the bags got wet they would expand and explode and sink the ship."

At that I laughed. I couldn't stop myself. I went into a kind of giggle fit, which someone driving by would certainly not think was proper for a widow with her neighbor on her porch.

I laughed until I cried.

And then Thomas put his arm around me. I pulled away. Nobody but my husband had put his arms around me in eleven years. Except Pete, of course. Most of my students tend to be women, and occasionally they'll throw their arms around me at the end of the semester at the YMCA, but that's different, and even then I pull away. I try to relax my shoulders, but I never know what do with my arms.

I wiped my eyes. "I should see how Pete is," I said.

"How's he doing?" asked Thomas.

"By day he's okay, but at night he keeps asking if Ed is buried the same place dinosaurs are."

Thomas did not come to the funeral. He was away that weekend. I don't know if he was working or on a romantic retreat with his girlfriend, but I was not concerned with him at that moment, and I never found it strange. At the funeral, I was determined to be as brave as Jackie Kennedy. Pete didn't exactly salute, but he did take the shovel and help bury his father.

Thomas, according to local lore, had moved from down south. He moved in when Pete was two. The story was that he was divorced and had taken the job as cooper up at Hill House, because the last cooper, Jimmy Trotta, a boy I went to high school with, had been found dressed up as an eighteenth-century scullery maid, complete with layers of undergarments and lots of makeup, sitting on the bed in the master bedroom, eating Pringles. Jimmy moved out of town and soon after, Thomas arrived.

Thomas once told me at a block party that he had a master's degree in colonial Dutch history, but he liked to work with his hands.

The condolence cards I am receiving tend to be of two types, the "This is the worst tragedy that can ever befall anybody, and I don't know how you'll have the strength to get through this, life is so cruel" variety, and then there is the "I know you have the strength to get through this, and your son will help you carry on" variety.

To all of them I respond, "Ed and I were very lucky to have eleven wonderful years together, and Pete and I will now carry on."

Teaching saves me. It always has. The stories of my students fill me up like I'm taking the waters at some

European spa. Now I'm reading the story of one lady whose father was a furrier and washed his hands with lemons every night to get rid of the animal smell. I have taught in strange classrooms at the YMCA, but the one I'm in now is unique. It is called "The Log Cabin." The tiny room somehow has no windows, but it is literally lined with logs, and has a gingham checked curtain over a faux window. My only requirement for the class is that students be fifty years old, and only rarely do people lie about their age. Many of them are widows themselves. "My father wouldn't allow a radio in the house. He said they were a crazy fad," a ninety-two-year-old lady wrote. I've only been back at work a week now, and I have become one of them.

Today I woke up with a headache from the noxious smell of skunk. A moment later, Thomas banged on the screen door. I struggled for my bathrobe. Through my sleepy eyes and the screen I could see him holding a wood and chicken wire cage he'd obviously made.

Pete joined me immediately and started yelling, "Stinking skunk, stinking skunk!" and pushed open the door.

"Do you want to help find the skunk?" Thomas said, and Pete immediately took his free hand.

As they marched down the porch steps together I could hear Pete say something about "killed animals." I know that when he finds out where hamburgers come from, he'll become a vegetarian. Last year a friend stayed with Ed and I took Pete to the little Natural History Museum out on the highway, and he hated it. "It's just full of killed animals," he said. "I want to leave." So we raced home.

It's the mornings that are the most difficult for me. Thinking about the Wright brothers helps. It's my little drug, those boys who had the bicycle shop in Dayton. I sneak out any book from the library that remotely mentions the brothers. When Ed got sick, I first indulged my fantasy of spending the summer of 1903 with them at Kitty Hawk. In truth, I had distant cousins who lived there, Sara and Alvin Trovsky.

Last night I dreamed the brothers appeared, in their suits and derby hats, at the house on their bicycles, and I could feel myself blush under the long peach dress I wore. Wilbur, the elder was a bit stern, and put his arm protectively on Orville's shoulder. Orville had a beautiful thick mustache.

We shook hands, all of us crisscrossing arms like we were going to do some kind of awkward square dance on the porch.

We had a fish dinner and fresh pumpernickel bread that Sara had baked. The sink was full of oyster shells and crab legs and fish eyes. Before they left after dinner, Orville tipped his hat and said, "Miss Hanna, it would be an honor if you came and looked at our machine."

I was washing out Pete's sneakers in the kitchen sink, recalling this dream, while I watched Thomas and

Pete stalk skunks in our backyards with the cage. Thomas's white hair makes him look older, although his skin is quite smooth. I know he is not fifty yet, because when Ed was still alive and we were all standing in our front yards, Ed had said, "I don't know if I'm going to celebrate half a century."

I didn't know what to say, so I said, "I want to go to Kitty Hawk for my fiftieth birthday."

"Sounds good to me," said Thomas, and Ed had put his arm around me.

Ed's forty-fifth birthday, his last, was not a happy day. Pete had meticulously wrapped eleven gifts, mostly trucks, a yo-yo, and some rolls of Scotch tape. He presented them to Ed, who could barely speak at this point, and said, "I'm saving some for next year when you're forty-six."

This was the day when Pete burst into tears and said, "Take off my training wheels, take them off now," but Ed couldn't wield a screwdriver anymore, and we knew that he couldn't help Pete steer anyway, but mainly we knew, all of us—Ed with his scrambled head, me with my weeping eyes, and Pete in his infinite four-year-old wisdom—that his father would not be around to see him learn to ride his two-wheeler without training wheels.

· · ·

This week's assignment for my students was a memory of shoes. "My grandparents were both blind and wore high-button shoes. They came to this country from Hungary when they were fifteen and were married for seventy years," wrote one woman.

"My father was a carpenter in South Africa. He left raw planks of wood out in the yard. When it rained, the smell of sweet cedar and his work boots filled the house," wrote another. Ed's mother made the children take off their shoes in the parsonage after dinner each night and march around the table on a rough hemp rug, carrying Bibles on their heads.

Pete has been hiding in Ed's closet lately, sitting on his father's shoes. I suppose he's planning his contribution to the great time line of history. Lately he's told me, "I want to bring Mimo to my job when I grow up."

"What's your job going to be?" I asked him with my back to him as I washed our few dishes.

"Astronaut and also hot-dog man."

I had wanted another child with Ed. We were trying, as they say, when he was diagnosed. I first wanted a child when I was six years old, and then did not think about it again until the limelit day I graduated from high school, when the boys coaxed a cow up the stairs. The cow stood simply among the sewing machines for forty-five minutes before it was discovered. The football team had to carry the cow back down the stairs. Two hours after the cow incident, I left town and drove out to Minerva, Ohio, where I spent the summer with my surprised kosher grandparents and their clove-and-cinnamon bakery.

Last night it rained lightly, and this morning when I went out to get the newspaper, it was furled like a damp fish on the lawn. I had a sensation that when I went back in the house, I would find Ed at the kitchen table, drinking coffee.

Of course he was not. Instead, I walked in and heard Pete crying from his bed. "Why did you leave?" he sobbed.

I kissed his forehead and he was hot as a baked potato.

"I just went to get the paper . . ."

"Don't leave me alone, ever. When are you going to die? Who will take care of me when you die? I don't ever want to go to sleep-away college."

"I'm not going to die for a long time."

"Could Thomas take care of me, and I live at his house?"

Pete was not crying now, but he was still burning up. He wouldn't be able to go to day camp, and I had to teach.

"Stay here, baby. I'll get some children's aspirin."

"Don't leave me," he said.

He climbed onto me like a monkey, clinching his little legs around my waist. I hobbled to the medicine cabinet, holding him with one hand, reaching for the children's ear thermometer. I clicked it on and stuck it in his ear.

"You can't go to camp today. You have a-hundred-and-three temperature."

"What's temperature? Will you stay home?"

"No, I have to work. I'll call Andrea or Mattie," his two favorite baby-sitters.

It was a half hour before I had to leave.

I spooned some cherry children's Tylenol into Pete's mouth, half of which he spit out on my shirt, and then I called the sitters. Neither was home. They're students, and what could I expect, but I couldn't miss work, and I couldn't leave Pete alone with raccoons as his keepers. When I went back in to him with a wet washcloth for his head, he said, "I want my tall Daddy. I want my tall Daddy now."

"I have to get to work. Who do you think could watch you?"

"Thomas," said Pete, throwing the washcloth on the floor.

I do not know Thomas's exact schedule up at Hill House, but there are days that he dresses in colonial garb, and days that he's just in T-shirts and jeans. Ed thought the Hill was a farce, not historically correct. There were always rumors about the place. In the brochure for Hill House it says, "Hill House was established in 1952 to re-create the lives of eighteenth-century colonists, to help us learn from the past to build a better future." At that time, there were rumors that the place was run by Communists. When I was a kid there was vague talk of a cult. But that was not the point. Now I needed a baby-sitter.

I quickly got dressed in my schoolmarm clothes—
long navy-and-white skirt and a half-ironed white blouse
and sandals, my hair back in a ponytail. I even wear
my glasses on a chain around my neck, a beaded chain,
that Ed got me and I like very much.

I went back on the porch to think. There was Thomas, with his cup of coffee, standing at the railing of
his porch. He did not turn to look at me.

"Where's Pete?" he said, not turning his head.
"Doesn't he go to Whippoorwill?"

"He's got a fever," I said.

"I'm in the twenty-first century today. I can watch
him." He did turn his head when he said this. If he
had not looked at me when he said this, I would not
have left my son.

But he did turn, and I'm not sure why, but I said,
"You are a very kind person."

"My ex doesn't think so," he said. "Where's the pa-
tient?"

He walked down his steps, across both our yards and
up our steps.

I was a little nervous to leave Pete with him, and to
have a man so close to me on my porch.

I turned and held the screen door open behind me.

"Would you really do it?" I said. "I can get back by
three today."

"I said I could," said Thomas, marching into Pete's
room. "So," I heard him say, "do you want me to pour
ice cubes on your head?"

Pete laughed through his fever.

I said, "there's food in the frigerator."

"We'll be okay. You'll be late," said Thomas.

I kissed Pete's forehead. "Thomas will stay with you."

"I know that," he said, pulling away from me.

"Bye," I called as I went to grab my bag. "Bye," I called from the porch, but neither of them replied.

One day, when Pete was three years old, and Ed was walking around healthy and all was right with the world, I had a male colleague from work over for dinner. I was wearing a short skirt.

As soon as I changed into my good clothes, Pete said very loudly, "Why are you wearing vaginas?"

I remember the stricken look on Ed's face.

"Excuse me?" I stumbled.

Of course, the child just repeated the question, this time even more loudly, just as my colleague was making his way up the porch steps. I didn't know him well enough to make a joke about it. Instead, we all had a drink and pretended we hadn't heard, and Ed tried to distract Pete by blasting a Raffi tape of "Baby Beluga."

When I'm home and Pete's at school or day camp, I feel a jittery uneasiness all day. When I'm at work and he's at school or day camp, I feel like I'm missing a foot. When I'm at work and he's at home, which used to happen with Ed on occasion, it was fine.

Now here was Thomas, the neighbor doing God knows what to entertain the sick boy. Joya said that under no circumstances would she hire a male baby-sitter for her daughter or her son. The statistics on child-molesting men were off the charts, according to her. She would get very worked up over this issue.

After I finished teaching, I ran out of the classroom, stumbling and dropping my notebook and papers as I went. After I frantically scooped them up, I told my students that they could call me if there was a question. In the car I did not put on my seat belt and the damn warning beeper beeped all the way home as I raced through a yellow light. When I finally skidded home, I parked, but left the door open, and then I ran up the porch steps.

Thomas was sitting on the couch, watching a Reds game. Pete was lying with his head on his lap and said, "He let me lick batteries."

I grabbed Pete from Thomas.

"What? What?" I sputtered.

Thomas shook his head. "I changed the batteries in his dolphin flashlight, because they were dead, and I let him put his tongue on the old battery. It gives a funny buzz to your tongue. I told him never to do it on new batteries."

"Could it hurt him?" I said, stroking Pete's feverish forehead.

"No, it's fine. You want to try?"

"Great," I said, shaking my head. "Was Pete okay?"

"I got him to eat some soup."

"Thomas said I can use his real saw when I'm better," said Pete. "Actually when I'm six."

"Maybe ten," I said, lying him down on the couch.

"Well, thank you, Thomas, thank you very much," but Thomas was watching the game.

I hurried into my bedroom, shut the door, and put on some pants and a sweatshirt. I needed new bras.

When I came back out, Thomas was gone.

Pete's fever spiked in the middle of the night up to 104, but I didn't call the doctor. Ed's illness and death has made me a little daft. Sometimes I think life is all random, and there's nothing you can do about anything, and I let Pete eat chocolate ice cream for breakfast. Other times I worry if he is a little washed-out looking, and I'm convinced he has leukemia. I suppose this stuff calms down, but maybe not. In the middle of the night, I made the decision my son wasn't dying, and just brought him into bed with me and put cool washcloths on his forehead. He's very sweet when he's sick, lying on me like we're posing for a Madonna and baby Jesus sculpture. Finally at 5 A.M., he fell asleep. I did, too, and I called in sick to work.

At 10 A.M., there was a knock on the screen door. I unwrapped Pete from me, pulled on my bathrobe, and made my way to the door, rubbing my eyes.

It was Thomas, and he was wearing his colonial muslin clothes, the billowy shirt and loose trousers. His belt was made out of some kind of hemp, I imagine.

"Good morning," said Thomas. "I noticed you didn't go to work. How's Pete doing?"

"His fever's okay. I don't think he'll die," I sputtered. "I mean, I'll call the doctor if it goes on another day, but I imagine it's just one of these viruses."

Now Pete had stumbled out of bed and was standing next to me, rubbing his eyes.

"Hi, sergeant," said Thomas.

"Why are you wearing those clothes?" said Pete.

"This is what I wear when I work. Do you ever go to the Hill?" he said, looking straight at me.

"Not since I was a kid, class trips. How many days do you work there?"

"Just two. I also make barrels for some of the distilleries. My father was a barrel maker."

Pete looked up at him and said, "My father was a teacher, but he died."

I did not know where to look, but Thomas opened the screen door. He put his hand on Pete's hot forehead and said, "I know. He was a great guy."

As Ed's mind frayed, Pete learned to talk, as if Ed's wisdom was being emptied into Pete's head.

I keep finding lists I made in June.

1. name tapes for camp
2. hats (to cover Ed's baldness and one for Pete to copy him)
3. finish writing wills
4. yo-yo's for twins
5. mail Ed's driver's license renewal (which would be valid for the next five years)

Now, with Thomas so close, and Pete pulling on his hand, I was compelled to go into the living room and sit down.

"Do you have it now? Do you have a fever?" Thomas came over and sat next to me on the couch.

"No, no, I'm fine. Thank you."

Pete came in and put his head down on my lap. "Are you going to die?"

"No, no, I'm not going to die."

"You need a new bulb for your refrigerator," said Thomas. "I noticed it when you were at work. I'll be gone tonight. I have to go down to a distillery, but I'll be back late tomorrow. I'll bring one then."

"Thank you," I said. "Thank you very much."

"Where are you going?" said Pete.

"To work. I'll be back tomorrow," said Thomas, and he bent down and rubbed Pete's head, which was nestled in my lap.

"Thank you," I waved. "Thank you very much."

Pete ran to the window to wave at him, and I stayed slumped on the couch.

I heard him drive off in his pickup truck, but Pete stayed waving at the window.

"I'm going to wait for him here," he said.

"You're sick. You should be in bed," I said.

"I'm waiting here," said Pete.

I lay down on the couch. I did have a fever. I was burning up. That day was a blur, and that night insomnia was my Lord God. Pete's fever was high but not dangerous, and he slept in patches, but I thrashed around on the living room couch, with the kitchen radio turned on low to a country-and-western station. And then, to cool myself off, I went out on the porch, just in my nightgown, and sat on one of the rockers, rocking back and forth like a madwoman.

Pete was crying out in his sleep, but as soon as I stood up, he settled himself. I sat back down on the rocker. I sat twisting my wedding ring, and then I pulled it off and threw it into the bushes. I held out my hands in front of me. I could see their outline, my same child hands I had, the same old woman hands I will have if I'm lucky. I felt off-balance without my wedding ring on, but then I felt off-balance with it on as well.

I wondered if Wilbur and Orville had ever been in love with anyone but each other. In my fantasy, Orville has only loved me. With my wedding ring off I had the sensation that I had hopped on one of those first flying machines, running and running, and that I was up in the air, not in the sky, I would not say that, but in the air. The landing was rougher than I had imagined, smacking me squarely in the knee. They both ran to get me, both brothers, and Orville gave me a ride on the back of his bicycle, pulling my own bicycle along at the side. I sat sidesaddle and had to put my arms around his waist or I would have fallen off. I had no choice.

•   •   •

The windshield of our Honda cracked the day before Ed was diagnosed with brain cancer. When we got the news, Pete walked out to the front yard and put rocks in the hubcaps, so for about a week every time I drove there was a terrible sound of large rocks clattering around in the wheels.

This is what my fever felt like, except I really couldn't afford to take another day off from the teaching or the library. Pete watched television for eight hours. But the next day I rallied, as did he, and we both went off to our little worlds, he to Camp Whippoorwill, I to the YMCA.

When I got home, there was a powder-blue Mustang in neighbor Thomas's driveway. I laughed out loud, surprised that Thomas would trade his truck in for such a car. But, of course, it wasn't his car at all. He was in Tennessee delivering some wooden casks to a bourbon distillery.

I hurried up the porch steps and had the sense that someone was looking at me from his kitchen window, but I couldn't see anybody. I stumbled into the house and played the answering machine. One message from Pete's camp saying he said he was allergic to swimming and could I call them.

I threw my book bag down on the kitchen table and slumped into a chair. I wished I was at Camp Whippoorwill for the summer. Who drives a powder-blue Mustang, anyway?

I kicked off my sandals and leaned back and put my feet up on the table. That was one of the most difficult things I found about being a mother, was setting an example. I loved to put my feet on the table. And I liked to be able to walk from the bathroom to the bedroom without clothes on. Neither was advisable with Pete.

For the former, he began putting his feet up on the table, which he could barely do without tipping over the chair, and the latter brought forth a litany of "I can see your bretsis (his word for breasts), I can see your bretsis!"

But I did have these few minutes before he returned from camp. I took out the iced coffee I'd bought on the way home, sat with my feet up, and pretended I was on vacation. I wondered if Thomas really did have a secret girlfriend he visited. I remember the day he moved in, because he moved everything himself. There was no big van, and he had a lot of wood, raw planks, and partially built casks. Ed had made a comment at the time about him being a bootlegger. We didn't know he was a cooper up on the Hill.

Once a year there were block parties, and Thomas would show up in his muslin clothes and drag a workbench and lathe out into the middle of the street and demonstrate how to make wooden bowls. I always liked the smell of the wood. Once he gave Pete a tiny wooden box full of marbles, which I thought was sweet, but made Ed mad because he said any fool would know not to give a two-year-old marbles.

I broke a dish as I placed it in the dish drainer, and it shattered to the floor. I immediately went to the mud room and found a pair of big rubber boots to put on and then returned to the kitchen to sweep. There I was in my cotton frock and big rubber boots, when there was a knock on the door. I swept up the last slivers of glass, dumped them in the garbage, and went to the door with the broom in my hand.

I could see a young woman through the screen, with a blond ponytail. She was smoking a cigarette. I cared most about the cigarette, because if Pete saw a cigarette, which he called "sig-rat," he'd start yelling at the person.

"Do you know where Tom is?"

Just then Pete's bus pulled up, and he came running out. He froze when he saw the cigarette. I could see it all through the haze of the screen. It looked like Pete was playing an odd game of freeze tag.

"Pete!" I called. "Come inside. It's okay." To the young woman, I explained, "I'm sorry, my son's scared of cigarettes. My husband just died. Would you mind putting it out?"

The young woman squinted her eyes really small and dropped the cigarette on the porch floor.

She was twisting her foot on it as Pete yelled, "That lady's starting a fire!"

I pushed open the screen door and ran down the steps to Pete. He was crying now, and I picked him up. "It's okay, it's okay. She's a friend of Thomas's."

The young woman was coming down the porch steps now. She was wearing a tight turquoise T-shirt with no bra and perfect little breasts, a bare midriff with a ring in her navel, and short shorts. She was barefoot and looked like she rarely wore shoes.

"He's not my friend," she said, and she went back to his house.

"I hate Thomas," said Pete, stomping into the house.

All my life I have yearned for inner tranquility. If someone had just held up his or her hand when I was four years old and said, "Missy, you'll never have it, now move along," it would have saved me some bother. There was a girl named Holly Hillier in my class at school, and her parents were born-again. The whole family went to an island in the Caribbean and was gone most of the year. Holly returned with her hair lighter and her skin darker, and she bought a stalk of sugar cane to show the class for show-and-tell. The rest of us stood clutching our pennies and yo-yos and robin feathers, while Holly, in all her blonde glory, stood proudly with her magnificent treasure. Holly passed the magic wand around the circle and nobody worried about hygiene. All the kids stuck out their tongues and had a lick. When we started jumping, we were so excited, our teacher, Miss Lancaster, said, "Girls, let's have some tranquility in here."

Now, with Pete in a snit because there was a young

woman he called a lady who was smoking a "sig-rat" on our porch, I chanted to myself, "Let's have some tranquility. Let's have some tranquility."

"C'mon, Pete," I pleaded, as Pete hurled himself onto the couch. Who was this girl?

Green jealousy knotted up in me at unpredictable times all my life. Pete was talking now. "Boys go to college to get more mileage. Girls go to Jupiter to get more stupider."

"I don't approve of the sentiment," I said, "but I believe the correct words are, 'Boys go to college to get knowledge,' not mileage."

"No, it's mileage," said Pete.

"Fine, how are you feeling?"

He did not respond.

"Well, what do you want for dinner?"

Meals used to be almost normal when Ed was alive, normal in that we did sit at the table together. But now I usually stand eating over the sink in the kitchen, while Pete watches TV.

"Fish sticks, hot dogs, or alphabet noodles?"

"Apple," he said.

"You can't just have an apple. I'll make fish sticks."

"No, hot dogs."

"Fine," I said, as I went to the kitchen and peered out the back window. I couldn't see the girl. I wondered if I should invite her over for dinner. I turned and stood staring at the refrigerator. There was a card sent by a cousin after Ed died. It was held up with a motorcycle magnet. "For all are born and all shall die. Life's all the time left in between—to follow a star—to build a dream."

I opened the freezer, and three frozen hot dogs spilled out on the floor. I picked them up, stuffed two back in the box, closed the freezer door, and set the water to boil. I rarely ate what Pete ate. That's not true. I often ate his leftovers. I lost my appetite when Ed stopped eating when he did his radiation, and haven't gotten it back.

Just then I heard a car screech out of the driveway next door. I ran to the front door carrying the one frozen hot dog, as the powder-blue Mustang drove off.

At 4 A.M., after a restless sleep, I crept downstairs. I had the urge to cook for the first time in two years, and I whipped up a batch of gingerbread. I stirred like a dervish as the smell of cinnamon and ginger filled the room.

I felt compelled to cook gingerbread. There happened to be heavy cream in the refrigerator that I'd bought to make a cake for Pete's camp group, the Badgers, but I had barely been able to buy cupcakes at the supermarket at the time. I smelled the cream. It was still good, and I set to whipping it into frothy peaks while the gingerbread baked. Then I bent down and licked the stuff, my face in the bowl like an animal.

I went back outside to sit on the porch. I was desperate for a parcel of sleep. There was a hint of autumn in the air, like when I was a child and ironed individual leaves into waxed paper bags, filling the kitchen with the smell of melting wax and maple leaves. But now it was still the dog days of August. A cow was mooing in the valley. At first it sounded like the cows usually did, like the daytime cows lazily walking in the fields, but as the mooing bellowed on, I heard something haunting in that bellowing. I jumped up and paced back and forth tacking across the porch. I had never heard that exact sound before, but Joya had told me about it. She had a bad brother, Charlie, who used to tip cows with his friends late at night. I never could imagine having a brother of my own, so I listened to the exploits of Charlie with particular concern.

Tipping cows was something rowdy teenage boys did after they'd drunk a six-pack or two. The hoody boys drove out of town, deep into the hills in a rusty-holed pickup truck that looked like it was made in medieval times. They drove far past the Hill. Then, as I understood it, Charlie raised one dirty-fingernailed hand. He whispered, "On the count of three," and on "three," he lowered his hand and the gang pushed over the sleeping cow. When the cow landed, it made a deep and howling sound. That is the sound I heard in the gray-light hours of my insomnia. I prayed Pete would not become a hoody boy.

I worried about Pete. He often came home from Camp Whippoorwill with a sticker on his shirt that said "Ask me about Dodge Ball" or "Ask me about Zip-

Line," and every time I dutifully asked he answered, "I didn't do that," or, "We never played that."

I sat wondering if Thomas had ever tipped cows. I was asleep on the porch swing when he drove up the driveway. It was still dark. It must have been 5 A.M. I could feel him standing over me before I saw him.

"I got the refrigerator light," he whispered.

I rubbed my eyes. I looked up and he said again, "I got the refrigerator bulb."

"Thank you," I said, as if we were having a normal conversation. "Thank you very much." I wanted to stay lying down but I sat up as straight as I could.

He handed me a small paper bag.

"Thank you," I said again.

"I got it in Tennessee. Everything's cheaper there."

I nodded. I had it in my head to tell him that a young lady with a navel ring had visited very briefly, but somehow I thought he needed some sleep before he got that news, or at least daylight.

I sat swinging quietly on the porch swing, and he stood there, looking out at the sun beginning to thread through the trees. Finally, I said, "Did you ever tip cows?"

"Yes, I did once."

"Why do boys do it?" I said. "Don't tell Pete you did it."

"We like to stir things up. D'you think I'm a bad influence on your son?"

"I didn't mean to criticize," I mumbled, as he walked down the porch steps. "Thank you for this," I said in a loud whisper, holding up the little bag.

He bowed, or made a kind of bow, in the front yard, and then went back over to his house. I went inside and did not call him about the girl. I stood at the kitchen sink, letting cool water run on my wrists. I figured that since the earth was four billion years old and men and women had been trying to wiggle around together gracefully for 400,000 years, life should have evolved less peculiarly. It was not that I was just confused. I was concerned that I might do something bad, like tip a cow. I was frightened that I would quickly go out of my mind, put a wad of paper into the toaster instead of toast, and burn the house down, as simply as going down to the cellar for a sack of potatoes and then suddenly somersaulting down the stairs. As the sun rose, I unscrewed the old refrigerator bulb and replaced it with the new one. The light going on in the refrigerator filled me with inexplicable joy.

Now Pete was calling me and I went to him.

"Why did dinosaurs die?" he mumbled.

"I don't know. Now go to sleep." I lay down next to him and rubbed his back.

I lay there wide awake, thinking he was asleep, when he said, "Mom."

"Go to sleep," I pleaded.

"You know when there's a river and it's regular, sweet water, and then my counselor says it turns salty before God takes it to the ocean."

"Pete, you have to sleep a little more."

"Why? It's morning."

The child was right. The sun was pouring in.

I stood up. "I have to feed the cat. What do you want for breakfast?"

"Pancakes."

I do like to make pancakes, from a mix, Aunt Jemima. One egg, tablespoon of oil, cup of milk. God is in heaven.

I stirred up the batter, and was pouring it into heart-shaped pancake molds Ed and Pete had picked out last Valentine's Day, when I heard someone on the porch. One winter a baby deer clambered onto the porch, before Pete was born, and we sat in the living room, Ed and I, peering from behind the couch at the sweet animal. This was not a baby deer.

"Hello? Hanna?"

Thomas came walking into the kitchen. His hair was wild. He looked like he had slept facedown on a knobby bedspread. He was wearing the same rumpled clothes he'd driven home from Tennessee in.

"The refrigerator work alright?" he asked, opening the refrigerator door.

"Yes, thank you," I said, flipping a pancake. "Would you like one?"

"Yes, please."

I flipped two heart-shaped pancakes onto a plate and offered him a chair. He made no comment on them, but picked up his fork and started to talk.

"Did you see someone? When I was gone?"

I nodded, then turned away from him and looked

out the window. "Yes, a young woman, a girl I guess, in a powder-blue Mustang."

I heard him drop his fork and turned to look at him. He was staring past me, toward the sink. My husband used to get that look sometimes, and I could never read it completely, a look I think he didn't want me to fully comprehend. Now Pete wandered in with a knock-hockey stick in his hand, throwing a tiny tire from one of his toy trucks in the air. He swung wildly at the tire, dropped it, and kept repeating this game.

"Good hit," said Thomas when the tire sailed into the pancake batter.

"Do you say, 'Good morning'?" I said to Pete, picking the gooey tire out, rinsing it, and handing it back to him.

"Someone you know?" I said to Thomas, referring to the Mustang.

His response was, "Hey, can I have a turn at that?" talking to Pete.

Pete ran out of the room shouting, "I'll get you the other one."

"What about pancakes?" I said. "Isn't anybody going to have breakfast?" but now both of them were in the living room playing badminton over the couch with the little wooden sticks and the tiny tire. I stood with my spatula in the air and opened *Widows of the World* with my other.

"The wives of even poor Ibibios must remain secluded for a week after their husband's burial. During this time they may wear no garment save a small loin-cloth and a piece of goat's skin tied over the right hand."

I had burned a batch of pancakes. I flipped them over as they sizzled black, then threw them into the garbage. I stood, spatula raised again, staring out into the backyard.

"Can you take the training wheels off my bike?" I heard Pete say.

"Sure," said Thomas.

"Let's do it now."

"You have camp today," I called. "Do you guys want pancakes?"

"I want to skip camp."

"We'll do it when you get home," said Thomas, and they both returned to the kitchen.

I made up a fairly civilized batch of pancakes and stood over them like a mother hen as they ate. None of us spoke.

Thomas left, and I made Pete's lunch, stuffed it into his backpack, and hurried him out the door just in time for the bus.

Five minutes after he left, the phone rang. "So what did she look like?" It was Thomas.

"Who?"

"The woman in the Mustang."

"Pretty. Blonde. Young. I don't know. She had a ring in her navel."

"What?"

"Belly button, whatever you call it."

I could see Thomas out in his backyard with his cordless phone. He was bending down to do something as we spoke, and it took me a minute to realize he was yanking out weeds.

"Why did you see her stomach?"

"She had one of those little shirts."

"Christ!" he muttered and threw the phone down in the yard.

I hung up and went out the back door and stood there with my arms crossed as he continued to weed. Finally I said, "I have to go to work now. Are you okay?"

"Yeah," he said, "just fine."

That evening, when Thomas got back in his colonial clothes, Pete marched over there, pulling his two-wheeler, and I know Pete asked him to take the training wheels off his bike. I did not hear the conversation. I pulled the curtain on the side window and I could see the two of them bent over the wheels with screwdrivers, talking about God knows what, and I envied them, their Wilbur and Orville closeness. When I was a child, I loved to ice-skate with my friend Edna down the street. We would hold hands and glide across the ice, when it was cold enough, and when it was not, we slid across her parents' vast polished bedroom floor in our stocking feet, while we chanted the names of butterflies—Indian Glasswing, Blue Pansy, Northern Cloudywing, Silver Spotted Skipper, Silvery Checkerspot, Meadow Fritillary. I loved Edna, but she moved away.

Now Thomas stood up holding the training wheels like trophies high above his head, and Pete was wobbling down the sidewalk screaming, "I can ride a two-wheeler, I can ride a two-wheeler!"

I ran out to the porch to see Thomas running after him.

Pete yelled, "Don't hold me, don't hold me!" as Thomas grabbed his seat.

Thomas let him go and he rode for a few more seconds before he crashed.

As soon as I saw he was alright, I burst into tears, because Ed was not there to see it, and because it was not Ed's hand that let him go. I hurried into the bathroom and filled the sink with cold water, then dunked my head several times.

The night of the day Pete learned to ride his two-wheeler, Thomas appeared on the porch at 6 P.M., holding up a gallon of chocolate ice cream.

Pete was inside watching the same Blue's Clues video he was watching when his father died.

"The kid is good," said Thomas. "Great balance."

"He has to have dinner first," I said smoothing my hair at the door. "Thank you."

"Sure," and he opened the door and handed me the ice cream.

"I have to go up to the Hill. They're doing some demonstration for kids. Would you like me to take Pete? Give you a break?"

"What? Oh, no, no thank you."

Pete was at the door. "Do you want to go see how they made barrels in the olden days? And candy, there's an olden-day candy maker," said Thomas.

"I'm going," said Pete, and he pushed open the door.

"But, are you sure?" I sputtered.

"We'll be home by eight. They'll have dinner there. Ice cream after."

"Olden-day food," I said. "Okay, have fun."

Then I was alone in the house watching the damn Blue's Clues video. I sat spooning small slivers of chocolate ice cream out of the container, smoothing over my tracks, hoping Thomas wouldn't notice. I was finally able to control myself and put the container in the freezer when the video ended. I sat on the couch as the video rewound. I could only rewind when Pete wasn't home. I imagined the olden-day candy maker was a woman.

I was asleep on the couch when they got home.

Pete was standing over me. "Are you alive or what? Are you alive?" he said shaking me.

"Your mother's just taking a nap."

"She shouldn't," said Pete. "Mothers shouldn't take naps."

I sat up and rubbed my eyes. "How did it go?"

"It was good," said Thomas. "D'you still have that ice cream?"

"Sure, I'll get it." I went to the kitchen and dished out three portions before he had the chance to see I'd already eaten.

"Or did you already have it?" he called.

"No, no," I said. "What did you see, Pete?"

"Butter."

I returned with the dishes of ice cream on a tray. I never used a tray.

"Here, sit. What butter?"

"There's a woman in the kitchen who churns butter," said Thomas. "And bread. He tasted homemade bread."

"It was stupid," said Pete, and he went off to his room.

Thomas and I sat quietly eating ice cream as Pete's melted in his bowl, and I daydreamed of churning butter, churning and churning until I had blistered hands. I dreamed of letting Orville and Wilbur lick butter from my fingertips.

The evening folded into night as Thomas and I sat there. It was time for the exhausting ritual of putting Pete to bed, but I couldn't make myself move. It was so quiet in his room I was sure he was doing some sort of damage.

Finally Thomas said, "They also serve rosewater ice cream and steamed brown sugar pudding up there. You should come sometime."

"Thank you," I said. I was missing Ed's hands. "I have to put Pete to bed now. Thank you for taking him."

We both got up at once, and I went to Pete's room. The lights were on, but he was sound asleep, on his back, clutching his ticket from the Hill in his hand. I pulled off his shoes and turned off the light. I wanted to take Ed by the hand and show him his son. He'd never fallen asleep with the light on like that. I went back to the living room, but Thomas was gone, so I sat on the couch, clicked on the television, and told Larry King that Pete had fallen asleep wearing his shoes, with the light still on.

Thomas was gone for two days after that. Pete went off to camp, and I went off to work each day, but for two nights when there was no pickup truck in Thomas's driveway, I read from *Widows of the World* to put me to sleep.

"It is the Jukun practice in Africa for female mourners to sleep in the hut of the deceased. Each morning large quantities of local beer are sent to them by relatives and friends."

For the next two days I sewed new kitchen curtains in my spare time. The old ones were dusty-yellow-and-white-striped from when I was pregnant with Pete. Now I choose a fabric of small orange butterflies. I do not have a sewing machine. I'm no Dolly Madison, but I did sew them by hand. Pete did not notice them until

I pointed them out, at which time he said, "They're beautiful, and girls like them, too."

I wonder how Pete would be different if his father were alive. He's being shaped differently, like a river that changes its course.

The other thing I did when Thomas was away was clean out Ed's filing cabinets while Pete was at camp. It gave me a headache to do it, and mostly it was old checks and meticulously organized electric bill records, but I did find one postcard from a girl or woman from before we were married that said, "I miss every part of your sweet self." The postcard was a picture of a replica of the Eiffel Tower built in Texas. I suppose I should have saved it for Pete, for him to learn more about his father, when he learned to read, but I stuffed it in the garbage with the old electric bills.

I took off early from the library one day while Thomas was still away and Pete was being picked up from camp by a friend. I paid a visit to the Hill.

Herds of schoolchildren were gathering as I stepped over the threshold into the mansion. I almost tripped as I entered the year 1798. A woman I recognized as a part-time cashier at the supermarket wore a long dress and muslin cap, and ushered me to the gift shop to purchase a ticket. The gift shop was full of beeswax candles and bags of an old pancake recipe like Thomas had left us on the porch, and small wooden windmills that it was possible Thomas had made. The place reeked of some kind of violet sachet. I paid for my ticket and hurried through the front hall and did not stop to admire the porcelain and fossils and feathers brought on sailing ships. There were no tours at this time, so I had time to dash around before the children descended. I made my way down steep wooden stairs to the low-beamed kitchen where a young woman with large breasts and long flaxen hair stood at the butter churn. She did not greet me.

Instead she kept churning, staring at the floor as she snapped, "My name is Robin, and I'm tired."

I nodded and nervously twisted my hair into a braid so it hung in a messy knot. Robin taught me more about butter than I ever thought I cared to know. The Hill had a five-gallon churn, which was kept half-filled with cream. First the cream had to "clabber," which was the old-fashioned word for turn. In summer it only takes cream a day to clabber, but in cold weather it can take as many as three.

After the cream clabbers, you churn for thirty or forty minutes, she told me, but I wasn't going to wait around for that. Robin pointed out the pipes that had been added to bring in water and the electric lights camouflaged behind the copper pans. Ed had a theory that everybody who worked up there was running from something.

I briefly considered applying for a colonial job. I didn't know how to churn butter, but I could make gingerbread. Pete wouldn't mind playing in the fields, although they make children of employees wear colonial garb, and I doubt he would give up his Velcro sneakers.

And then Robin flung her arm toward the small window and said, "After the kitchen you can go out the back door and take a tour of the outbuildings, the blacksmith's shed, the cooper's cabin, and the barns."

I put up my hand to my hair and tried to picture living two hundred years ago without electricity, without indoor plumbing, without a tormented brain. I thanked Robin, and just made it outside before the stampede of children came down the stairs.

The blacksmith, who looked the part, complete with heavy beard and crooked teeth, was pounding away on his anvil as I came by. He was talking "in character" as they say. "Morning, miss, some wagons from the East are due any day with some fine linens and teas you might enjoy."

I nodded and watched him clang away. There was an arrow pointing along the path to the cooper's shed. I stayed long enough not to be rude in any century, then thanked the man and headed down the path. The cooper's shed was a small, sturdy building that was locked. I peered in the window and could see several barrels, a workbench, and tools neatly hung on the wall. It looked the way Thomas's garage did, although of course there was no pickup truck. I'm not sure what I was looking for up at the Hill.

What I do know is that when I left, I hurried down the long driveway from Hill House. The sun shone a pale yellow on the fields, and the cows were in a sleepy haze, knowing that autumn would soon be here. It was not my plan, but I stopped at the Stop & Shop to buy large quantities of small bags of junk food for Pete's kindergarten, which would begin in two weeks. This comforted me. Kindergarten had always seemed so far away when he was a baby, and now he would be trekking off to the bus with a backpack. I wondered how the Wright brothers even went to kindergarten. It is difficult to believe that Wilbur missed both World Wars, while Orville endured the two of them. Perhaps Wilbur would not have been able to tolerate them anyway. He died in 1912 at forty-five. I passed the Slow Children sign as I turned into our road and had the thought that I was one of the slow children myself.

I parked in front of the house, ran up the porch steps, and threw the bags of snacks on the kitchen table. I had fifteen minutes before Pete got home from camp. I had one week before he started kindergarten. Kindergarten had been traumatic for me. I had taken a bite of Ritz cracker and a sip of apple juice before saying, "God is good and God is great. Amen," and was sent to the principal's office, my sagging tights bearing the weight of my penance.

I took my shower, and was wrapped in a towel when Pete came bounding into the house. "I hate it when you wear that," he said. "Is kindergarten tomorrow?"

"No," I called from the bathroom. I had begun to cover my naked self since the evening two weeks before when he had sneaked into the bathroom, yanked

back the shower curtain, and thrown a handful of popcorn into the tub.

That night I held Pete on my lap on the porch, facing
the night like someone was going to take our photograph. Thomas's truck was not in his driveway. I had
been reading Plato at the library to calm my nerves.
He said the three models of spiritual perfection are the
saint, the soldier, and the sage, and obviously I was
none of these three.

"Did Daddy leave me anything for kindergarten?'

"Like what?" I said, rocking back and forth. I always
tried to talk evenly in these conversations, like we
were a normal family.

Just then Thomas screeched into his driveway, and
Pete ran down the stairs and outside to greet him.
They both returned, walking up the steps to our porch
hand in hand.

"You want to come with me to the Hill?" said Thomas.

"It's nighttime. It's almost time for Pete to go to
bed."

"I'm going," said Pete, running back to Thomas's
truck.

"I have to pick up some tools. We won't be gone
long. It's pretty up there at night."

"I can't," I said.

"It's not a date," said Thomas shrugging his shoulders. "Another time."

"I didn't say it was a date," I mumbled.

Pete had climbed onto the hood of the truck now.

"Get down from there," I screamed. I didn't like to scream. I would never have considered myself a screamer, but I shrieked at Pete at least once a day now.

He did not get down.

"Your mother told you to get down," Thomas said sharply, and Pete jumped off the hood.

Thomas drove off, and Pete informed me of my terrible mothering abilities. That August night I taught him how to whistle. We sat in the grass and I reached over to his mouth. I held his lips and said, "Like this, blow in or you can blow out."

We sat in the grass for two hours like that, until it turned dark and the crickets slowed their chirps, but still Pete could not whistle. When I thought he would fall over in the grass from fatigue, I carried him inside and propped him up on the floor with his back against the refrigerator. A few minutes later he whistled for the first time. He whistled his own rendition of "Oh Susannah," and when he got to "Don't you cry for me," I was so proud of him I burst into tears.

The next morning I heard him whistling in his bed when he woke up, like a little bird. I was at the kitchen sink, scrubbing the tops of all the pots with steel wool, as a way to soothe my soul, when Thomas reached up his hand and knocked on the window in front of my face.

I motioned for him to come in, and in the next instant he was at the table with his coffee cup that said, The More I Know about Women the More I Love My Truck.

"So what else about this girl," he said.

"How do you know her?" I said, with my back to him as I scrubbed at the sink.

"I don't. She must have climbed in the window. It sounds like my ex-wife."

"She's about twenty years old!"

"I guess not," he shrugged, "but she left a note on the refrigerator."

I turned to Thomas. I wasn't sure what I was supposed to say. "Do you want to tell me about the note?"

"No, it was nothing. I mean it said, 'I think we should talk.' She didn't sign it. That's how it was when my ex kicked me out. Just one morning at breakfast. 'We should talk,' as if we hadn't spoken for the past fourteen years."

"What did you say?" Now I sat down at the kitchen table.

He went and stood looking out the kitchen window. "I didn't say anything. She just said she couldn't communicate with me and she wanted me to leave."

Pete was calling from his bed, "Mom!"

I tried not responding, but as usual that just made him scream more, "Mom! Mom! I need you!"

"Excuse me," I said to Thomas.

I went into his room. He was lying in bed kicking the wall. "I've told you, if you want me, please come get me and talk to me in a regular voice," I said.

"Is one of the Beatles named Mark?"

"Mark? No."

"Well I wish Ringo was here now."

"Come on, it's the last week of camp. Time to get up."

I could hear Thomas talking now, although I could not hear what he said while Pete was discussing the Beatles. "I'll be right there," I called to Thomas.

"Pete, two minutes, I'll see you in the kitchen."

I returned to the kitchen and Thomas was standing at the refrigerator with the door open, apparently talking to himself.

"Marco Polo spent twenty-four years on his journey to the Orient..."

"Do you want something to eat?" I said.

"No," he said, shutting the door. "Tell me, did this young woman say anything to you?"

"Just that you weren't her friend."

"She said that?"

"When I said to Pete that she was a friend of yours, she said, 'I'm not his friend.'"

I did not want to make any comments about older men and younger women.

Just then the cat howled.

"Pete!" I screamed. "If you kill that cat, we're not getting another one!"

"Maybe you need something to eat," said Thomas, pointing to the refrigerator.

"Sorry, I'm a little wound up, I guess. The hospice people and the grief counselor said I might have fits of rage now."

"Did you before?"

"Yes," I said meekly.

Pete was dressed with his shirt on backward in the doorway. "I wish I was a Beatle. Then I wouldn't have to go to camp. If you're a Beatle do you have to go to camp?" he said.

"Absolutely," said Thomas. "The Beatles love going to camp."

We all ate cereal together like a pretend family. It was August 30. Labor Day approached.

"How old was she?" said Thomas, waving his spoon around like a child.

"Who?" said Pete.

"The woman in the Mustang."

"The woman who was smoking a cigarette," I added.

"Her lungs are going to get black and she'll die," said Pete.

I finally got Pete out the door to camp, and Thomas disappeared when I scooped up a pile of stuff for the dry cleaners that I'd been avoiding—Ed's winter coat, mine as well, and various items we rarely wore but that always seemed stained. I felt I had to get the house in order. Maybe someday Pete would wear his father's overcoat.

• • •

At the Spotless Cleaners, the Indian man, who looked in his thirties, with pumpkin-colored skin and coal-black hair, checked Ed's coat pockets. He didn't come up with any lipstick-stained handkerchiefs.

"My condolences for your husband," he said.

"Thank you," I said.

One ice-cold winter before Pete was born, Ed and I had gone ice-skating on Saw Mill Pond at night. The firemen had strung up lights for the town and I'd put my right hand in Ed's left pocket and we'd held hands that way, gliding around and around. I imagined holding the Spotless Cleaners man's hand.

"How's the boy?" the man said.

"He's fine. Children are resilient."

"Sometimes they are, yes," he said, checking more pockets.

"Do you have children?" I said, as he handed me the receipt.

"Yes, my son, he'll start kindergarten next week. How old is your boy?"

"Four and a half. Almost five."

"So is Omar."

"Maybe they'll be in the same class. There're only two kindergartens."

"Have a good day," he said. "Drive carefully."

Ed always used to tell me to drive carefully. Once I swear he told me to drive carefully, even though I was merely putting Pete to bed.

That night I was weary after teaching, but Pete was full of energy, as he usually is for fourteen hours of the day. I was lying on the couch when he ran in from the yard where he'd been digging, and yelled, "I can't get my sweatshirt off. I can't get my sweatshirt off."

"Calm down, calm down," I said sitting up.

"I have to go to the bathroom."

Pete liked to be completely naked when he went to the bathroom. God knows what he would do in kindergarten.

"Call Thomas!" he screamed. "Call him now."

"I can solve this," I said over and over. I grabbed the pliers from the top drawer. "I can solve this," I insisted, squinting at the zipper.

"You can't solve it!" screamed Pete. "Get Thomas!"

Then he ran out of the house sobbing, stuck in his sweatshirt, to Thomas's house. I had never been inside Thomas's house. I had been on the porch twice, once for trick-or-treating when Pete was dressed as a green worm and his costume ran in the rain, and once when Pete kicked a ball up the steps when Ed was too weak to leave the house.

I followed after Pete and knocked on Thomas's screen door. It was surprisingly sunny when I peered inside. I had pictured it to be a dark kind of cave. When I cupped my hands up to the screen, it looked like there was no furniture in the living room. I heard Pete sobbing still, and Thomas telling him to calm down.

"Hello," I called, and I let myself in. In fact there

was no furniture in the living room, just stacks of books piled on the floor in no particular order and a stack of wood piled neatly against the far wall. The place smelled of cedar. On the wall were black-and-white photographs of trees.

I hurried through the living room into a kitchen that was very sweet, with yellow-and-white-checked gingham curtains, like a woman's kitchen.

Pete was trying to wrestle away from Thomas, who was in his muslin clothes.

Thomas barked, "If you want to wear this thing for the rest of your life, keep crying. If you want it off, keep your mouth shut!"

Pete shut up, and Thomas unzipped the sweatshirt.

"Let's go to the batting cages," said Thomas.

Fifteen minutes later we were pressed into the cab of Thomas's truck, with Pete between us, on the way to Ben's Batting Cages. Thomas Jefferson might not have gone to Ben's, or even Leif Eriksson, but to the local Ohio men and boys, it was heaven on earth.

A man with a Reds hat stood behind the counter, in front of a wall plastered with baseball pennants. Mosquitoes zapped in the electric bug catchers hanging from the ceiling.

I surveyed the frenzy of baseball men in the heat. If you had very bad eyes, you could pretend there were real fans watching the batters in a real stadium. There was a painted mural on the back wall, full of cheering people. If you hit the ball to the top row, a red light would flash. And along with the joy of seeing the light flash, you got two free pitches, as well as a claim to fame at Ben's.

Thomas stepped up to bat in his colonial clothes, and he looked like he was jousting with several centuries. I stood quietly behind the fence, trying to restrain Pete, who insisted on climbing like a monkey, and each time I had to pull him off.

Thomas scored a home run on his second swing, and I jumped up and down. Pete shouted, "My turn, my turn," but I could see Thomas was taking this seriously.

Pete did get a turn, and connected with the ball once.

"Your turn," said Thomas, handing me a bat.

"No, no," I demurred. It didn't seem like a widow thing to do.

"C'mon, slug some of those demons out," he insisted.

I shook my head as I hugged myself.

Thomas and I were quiet on the way back, and Pete fell asleep on Thomas's lap.

When we got home, to both our homes, Thomas parked in his driveway and turned off the motor. He reached past sleeping Pete and took both my hands. "Your wrists are as small as plums," he said.

I pulled my hands away and gently lifted Pete off his lap. Somehow I managed to maneuver getting out of the truck without waking the child. It was a starry night.

As I went around the front of the cab, Thomas leaned out the window. "I'm going to Tennessee to-morrow—for about a week," he whispered.

I nodded and carried Pete into the house.

SEPTEMBER

The week Thomas was gone I spilled things, and the cat dumped Pete's chocolate milk all over the table twice.

During those days I got Pete's school supplies for kindergarten and a Curious George lunch box. I read my students' last stories of summer school, including Barbara Simon's, about her sister, who was playing field hockey on the beach in Germany when the Nazis grabbed her hockey stick and took her away.

The hospice worker called and asked, "How are you doing?" and I said, "I'm doing fine," but then I got off the phone and hurled a dish at the refrigerator, which shattered all over the place. I was angry that Ed would not be around for the first day of kindergarten or anything else. I was angry that my family was so small.

I could not sleep and stayed up reading *Widows of the World*.

When I did close my eyes, I imagined I was on a train to North Carolina, to Kitty Hawk, with my carpetbag overhead, on my way to visit the Wright brothers. The conductor called out, "Elizabeth City, Elizabeth City, North Carolina," in a singsong voice that sounded like a carnival. When I opened my eyes, I barely had time to wipe my brow with a handkerchief before the conductor had lifted down my bags. I took a short buggy ride to the dock for the voyage to Kitty Hawk Bay.

A fisherman named Mr. Lloyd, who looked like he was more comfortable transporting fish than people, tipped his hat and held out his hand as I stepped onto his rocking vessel. There was nobody else on board, just large stacks of mail and some stinking fish.

In fact Pete was shaking me awake, so I had slept. "Mom, how many days until kindergarten? I'll do kindergarten once, but then I'm coming home, nothing more, no first grade."

"Most schools in Ohio start in August. Ash Creek's different. You're lucky you don't start until now."

"I'll try one day of kindergarten, and that's it."

The first day of kindergarten was Monday, September 10. I was ready. Pete had his Curious George lunch box, filled with a bologna sandwich with ketchup, Oreo cookies, and an apple; small matchbox cars in each pocket; and an old green backpack of his father's. He was wearing a T-shirt with the front of a zebra on the

front and the back of the zebra on the back of the shirt
and shorts. His hair stuck up in the back like a duck,
but when I tried to smooth it, he swatted me. The only
way I got him out the door was when I promised that
he didn't have to go to first grade.

Thomas was still not back. I drove Pete that first
day. There was to be a parents' coffee in the playground after we pried the children off our legs. I wore
my teaching clothes.

Pete sat in the back of the car singing his rendition
of the Barney song, with the refrain, "We are a stupid
fam-i-ly."

When we got to the red brick school, where I had
gone, the Roaring Brook School, I parked and Pete
held my hand tight. All these fathers, even Kevin Mc-
Mahon whom I'd known as a boy, carried children on
their shoulders, which made Pete kick the dirt. I surveyed the family units with all their goddamn fathers.
And then I saw the man from the cleaners with his
little boy, Omar, who was wearing an ironed button-
down shirt and pressed long trousers with a belt.

I waved, Pete twisted my arm around behind me
and hid, while Omar and his father waved. I walked
over to them, dragging Pete. The mother was not
there.

Omar put out his little hand to shake and Pete said,
"No way."

But in a few moments they were chasing each other
around the flagpole with the American flag fluttering
in the breeze.

I stood with Omar's father. He smelled slightly of the cleaning fluid from the store. I liked standing close to him, and pretended we were a family.

"My wife is visiting her relatives, with the baby, in New York," he said. "Her brother works there."

"I've never been there," I said.

"It's wonderful," said Omar's father. "The Big Apple."

"I'm sorry," I said. "I know your son's name, but I don't know yours."

"Mazur," he said. "Please call me Mazur."

The school bell rang.

Pete and Omar ran into kindergarten holding hands and did not look back. I looked at Mazur.

"I have some clothes for you," he said. We edged our way over to the coffee table, piled with doughnuts and homemade cookies that people were too edgy to eat. All these kindergarten mothers and fathers stood around with name stickers on their chests, smiling and nodding, clutching coffee cups, worrying about sending their babes off to school.

People stand slightly farther away from me now that I'm a widow. Of course I don't carry a measuring tape around as proof, but I would say there's a good inch or inch-and-a-half more of a space. I did recognize a few women from Pete's preschool class, Daniella's mother, and Kathleen, the other single mother. They both murmured, "How are you doing?"

I had fifteen minutes before I had to go teach, and I felt myself pulling toward Mazur, but I saw him heading off to his van with Spotless Cleaners on the side, so I fled to my car and to work.

That day I missed Pete so much I threw myself into my students' stories at the Y. In a time of sound bites and Web sites, instant rewind and fast forward, their twentieth-century lives comforted me. We sat huddled in the Log Cabin room, and all was well until an argument ensued about Eleanor Roosevelt. Two women debated whether Eleanor should have spent more time with her children. I was able to steer them off that, and a tottering woman with pale blue hair, who had landed in Ohio via Vladivostok, eastern Siberia, raised her hand timidly. "I was born the year of the Russian Revolution. One evening my father bumped into Lenin on the street. Do you think this would make interesting stories? Yes?" For those hours I did not think about how Pete was doing, and whether he dared open his Curious George lunch box.

When the school bus dropped Pete at the house at 3:05, I was sitting on the porch as if I were waiting for him to come home from war.

"How was it? Did you like kindergarten? What did you do?" I opened my arms for a hug as he stomped up the steps.

He walked past me, dropped his backpack on the living room floor, went to his room with the cat, and slammed his door.

I followed him inside and talked through the door. "How was school?"

"Good," he said. "We had playground two times."

• • •

The next day, Tuesday, Pete hopped out of bed, and I had no trouble luring him out the door. It was a summer day slipped into September, no clouds, the leaves shimmering the way they're supposed to. The bus driver smiled and waved at me. Pete ran onto the bus. It was 8:15. I sat out on the porch with my coffee.

On the way to the YMCA, I listened to the radio, and there was some crummy news about a plane crash in New York City, so I switched the channel for country music, but every station had the same kind of frantic voice. "A tower has been hit. A tower has been hit."

By the time I got to the Y, I had gleaned that a plane had crashed into one of the World Trade Center towers, but I did not want to think about it. New York was in another solar system as far as we were concerned, although as soon as I entered the building, and saw everyone huddled around the TV at the front desk, I knew I was supposed to care.

All Classes Canceled, read a handwritten sign stuck hastily on the desk. I did not want to know what was going on. I did not want to look at the television. I heard the word *terrorist*, and I pictured Pete sitting on the floor in a circle for show-and-tell and figured terrorists weren't going to attack the Roaring Brook School, so I headed to the third floor to the swimming pool.

I sometimes grabbed a swim once a week after class, and this seemed like a little gift. I dove in, and as I swam I thought about Wilbur and Orville tinkering in their bicycle shop in Dayton, talking about flying like birds. There was a silence to the pool I'd never felt before. Usually the splashing of kickers using kickboards, or the show-off backstroke swimmers combined with the gossiping of the lifeguards echoed off the walls. Today was quiet, very quiet, but I swam my laps. All I wanted was life to be regular for Pete.

I swam, pulling through the water in my turquoise Speedo, fighting with the water, knowing I would have to get on land soon and face reality. Some people are blessed with a peculiar ability to feel two senses simultaneously, synesthesia it is called, or so I read on a slow day at the library reference desk. If they see the color red they might smell popcorn. If they taste a pistachio nut, they could hear Mozart, depending on the intricate way their particular brains are wired. The sensations are not necessarily rationally linked. What I felt now, as I lifted my head to breathe in the chlorine air, was Ed's hand in mine. At this point, the lone lifeguard screamed at me, "The YMCA is closing in five minutes! Please get out of the pool!"

I pulled myself up on the side of the pool and grabbed my towel. The lifeguard was struggling with his warm-up pants and did not look like he would save me if I dove back in again.

"What's happening?" I said, in a voice I thought was audible, but apparently was not. "What's happening?" I repeated.

"We have to evacuate. There's a bomb threat."

I ran through the shower room, then up the stairs to the locker room. I yanked on my clothes as fast as I could. Even if there was a bomb, I couldn't be seen outside in my thinning bathing suit.

Outside, people had scattered, and I caught up to my student from Vladivostok, walking very slowly to her car. "Are you okay?" I said.

She looked like she'd seen a ghost, and I thought it was because of my wet hair.

"Terrorists bombed the World Trade Center in New York City. Thousands of people are dead," she said. "I'm too old for this." She shook her head, and as I watched her drive off, I could see that she was crying.

I raced to my car now, and sat there listening to the radio. Then I turned on the motor and drove, slowly, very slowly to the Roaring Brook School. I parked in the parking lot and saw mothers running to the front door like in a cartoon, with their pocketbooks flying up in the wind. This was Pete's second day of kindergarten. I wanted him to have at least two days of school before he learned there was yet another way to die. I sat listening to the radio, then headed home to wait for him.

The sun was glaring bright now outside, but I went in to watch CNN. The towers were crumbling on the screen.

The telephone rang, and I snapped off the TV.

It was Thomas. "Are you alright?" He sounded like he was calling from underwater.

"Where are you?"

"Tennessee. Is Pete okay?"

"When are you coming home?" I said. "I mean, to your home . . ." I mumbled.

"I should be there tomorrow night," and then the phone went dead.

I was rocking fast on the porch rocker when Pete stomped up the stairs from the bus. "A plane of bad guys crashed into a control tower at the airport. Some kids got to leave school early. How come you didn't get me?"

Before I could answer, he had continued his journey into the house to search for the cat. Then he yelled, "Omar's daddy picked him up and he was crying."

I got up from the porch and followed him inside. "Who was crying?" I said.

"Omar's daddy," said Pete, clutching the cat.

"Why was he crying?"

Pete shrugged. "I think Omar hit him. Mrs. Irwin," the music teacher, who had been the music teacher when I was in school, "smiled really big and said we had to pray for everybody, even the bad guys."

"Are you okay?" I said.

"I didn't eat anything for lunch. The cafeteria smells."

"It smelled when I went there, but you'll get used to it."

"I won't."

The phone was ringing. Pete ran to answer it and

said, "ThisisPetewhoisthisplease?" the way he does.

He held the phone out to me. "It's a crying grown-up," he said.

I grabbed the phone. There was sobbing like a small dove, and it took a moment for me to make out that it was Mazur, Omar's father.

"Yes?" I said. "What is it? May I help?"

"My wife," he stammered, "my wife is there in New York," and then he was crying so much I couldn't understand at all, and Pete was jumping up and down.

"Can Omar come over? Can Omar come over?" yelled Pete.

"Her brother worked up there in those towers," Mazur said. "She was going to visit his office. I've been calling, but I can't get through."

"Do you want me to take Omar?" I said.

"Omar's coming over!" shouted Pete. "Omar's coming over!"

"Yes, please," he said. "I have your address on Algonquin, right?"

"That's right, Twenty-four Algonquin, just after the pond. He can stay as long as you like."

The boys spent the whole afternoon digging in the backyard, while I sat hunched on a chair in front of CNN, every so often getting up to watch them out the kitchen window. Whenever they ran in for cookies or the bathroom or whatever boys run inside for periodically, I clicked the television off.

This was the first sleepover for either of them, and they did not seem concerned with the world's events, except that before Pete fell asleep, he ran into my room and said, "If a plane crashes into our home, I'm throwing Mimo out the window. Then it would be okay to throw him out the window, right?"

I could not sleep a wink. I stood in front of the television, rocking back and forth on each foot. Every so often a car zoomed by, and I ran outside to the porch, holding the screen door open, waiting for peace on earth.

And then I ended up defrosting the refrigerator. I was still wearing my clothes, but I'd taken off my bra. I did a lot of cleaning the days after Ed died and gave serious if fleeting thoughts to opening a mourner's cleaning service. I was chipping away with a knife, which I of course know you're not supposed to do, when Thomas walked in at 2 A.M. It was September 12.

He was wearing a white T-shirt and blue jeans, and his white hair was rumpled the way it always seemed to be. He was wearing moccasins, real Indian moccasins. We did not say a word, and I felt like I was going to cry, so I turned my back to him and continued my chiseling. He grabbed me around the waist and held me that way tight, pressed up against my back. I kept chiseling, and he was touching my breasts, so I stopped.

Omar was calling from Pete's room. "Mama," and then I think he was crying something in an Indian dialect.

I pulled away from Thomas and went to him. Pete

was awake now. I flicked on the light, and they both were crying, holding onto each other. Thomas followed me, and picked up both boys and rocked them on the bed.

"It's okay," he said. "Did you guys ever hear the one about the fish that lived in a boy's bathtub?"

Pete stopped crying now, but Omar was hiccuping with tears.

"Omar's sleeping over," Pete said solemnly.

"I see that," said Thomas, lying both boys down. He took turns rubbing each of their backs. "Now the fish had a problem because he liked to go to school with the kids . . ."

Omar stopped crying. Thomas continued with the story for ten more minutes, and I went into the kitchen to cry into the sink. I could hear Thomas still talking. Nobody had touched my breasts except for Ed in eleven years, except when I nursed Pete.

When Thomas returned to the kitchen I'd stopped crying and stood facing him with my arms crossed tightly across my chest.

"Who's that kid?" said Thomas, as if he hadn't touched my breasts.

"His name's Omar. His father runs the dry cleaners. They're from India. His mother was visiting her brother in New York. The father drove out there to look for her."

I grabbed the knife again, and continued hacking at the ice.

Thomas went to the refrigerator and lifted a bowl of water from the bottom shelf, then slowly brought it toward me.

"Move over," he said, and dumped it in the sink. "You know you shouldn't use a knife."

"You shouldn't do a lot of things," I said, bending down to sponge up the floor.

The phone rang. I got it on the second ring. It was Mazur, and he was sobbing.

"I'm so sorry," I kept saying, and nodding my head. "Omar's fine here. Stay as long as you need to. The baby's okay? Good, good . . ."

He asked me not to tell Omar yet, that his mother was in the hospital. Her leg was broken. He hadn't gotten the whole story yet. The brother was definitely gone. The baby had stayed with relatives when they went to the towers.

"No, no, I won't," I said, shaking my head.

Thomas had the mop now and was cleaning around the refrigerator. The mop slipped and banged on the floor.

"Are the boys up?" Omar's father said through his sobs.

"No, no," I said. "I'm just cleaning. I couldn't sleep." Then I didn't know what to say, so I said, "I send my prayers."

When I hung up I said, "The mother's brother," and gave a thumbs-down sign. "The mother's in the hospital, but the baby's okay. I don't know when Mazur's coming back."

"Who's Mazur?" said Thomas.

"The father. I'm very tired now," I said. "I should get some sleep."

Thomas followed me into my bedroom, pulled back the covers, and I fell into bed with my clothes on. He was bending down to kiss me when his cell phone started ringing. I had no idea he had a cell phone.

"Hello?" he said quietly, the way a man who wore muslin clothes and carried a cell phone would.

And then he hurried out the door. I fell fast asleep, and didn't wake until I heard Pete or Omar spill the cat's bag of dry food all over the kitchen floor.

I jumped up and ran into the kitchen. The boys were somewhat dressed, although Omar had his shoes on the wrong feet. "My mommy is in New York, with my baby," he said to me.

Of course there wasn't any decent milk, because the refrigerator had been turned off.

"There's no milk," I said. "Would you boys like eggs?" I deemed the eggs were still good.

"I'm going over to Thomas's. C'mon Omar," but Omar sat down politely at the table, as Pete ran out.

I bent down and switched Omar's shoes as he ate scrambled eggs and said, "I've never had a sleepover before. My mommy's bringing me two presents when she gets back from 'cation."

Pete used the word 'cation for vacation, so I understood the boy.

"I'm sure she will," I mumbled as I stood up and

handed him a glass of orange juice. The school bus pulled up front and the driver honked, and quickly drove off.

I telephoned over to Thomas's house. "Hi, could you please tell my son that the bus just left, and I'll drive them, if he comes home immediately?"

Just as I said it Pete ran in the door, and Thomas said into the phone, "I need to talk to you."

"I have to get the kids to school," I said. "I'll call you later."

I hung up and asked Omar what he ate for lunch, assuming he ate some Indian food.

"Peanut butter and jelly," he said, politely wiping his mouth.

I made two lunches, marched the boys to the bathroom and combed their hair, then hustled them out onto the porch and to the car.

I drove to the Roaring Brook School with the radio turned on low, so that it was a quiet melody of the word *terrorist, terrorist, terrorist.* I glanced in the rearview mirror and I saw the boys holding hands. They were talking into each other's mouths, very loudly, about who had lost more teeth.

It was 8:45 when I got there, and the principal, Mr. Lofthouse, who had been a social studies teacher when I was there, wearing his bow tie and jacket, was closing the front door. I honked my horn and waved.

"Stop honking!" shouted Pete. "We'll get arrested."

Mr. Lofthouse waved and I was able to hurry the

kids in. If we were a minute later they'd need a late pass, which filled me with the same dread it did when I was in school. Beverly Ashley, whom I knew as Bev the beauty in high school, leader of the cheerleading squad, pulled up behind me and her three perfect children ran out.

After the kids were in, I parked the car and entered the building. I headed to the office down the familiar hallway that smelled of oranges and chalk.

The door to the office had a painted sign, Welcome to Roaring Brook, which had been made by fourth graders in 1958. Gladys, the nurse, the principal's secretary with a red beehive, and several other women I didn't know were huddled around a small television perched on one of the desks.

I beckoned to them both. "Please," I said.

Gladys came to the desk. "How are you doing? How's Pete?"

"Did you hear? Omar's mother is in the hospital. His uncle was killed," I said. I realize I didn't even know their last name.

"Who?"

"The dry cleaner. The mother might have been in those towers. She was visiting in New York. The little boy's in Pete's class . . ."

As I left the school, I could hear Principal Lofthouse leading the children in the Pledge of Allegiance over the intercom.

I raced to the YMCA, and when I could not bear to

hear about people jumping out of windows any longer, I turned off the radio and sang, "Row, Row, Row Your Boat" at the top of my lungs. As I hurried into the YMCA building, I was humming, "life is but a dream."

My students were agitated that day. Three did not show up. I tried to achieve some normalcy by having them write about a memory of a kitchen table from childhood, and as they did I found myself writing *Thomas the cooper Thomas the cooper* over and over in my notebook like a schoolgirl. I scribbled it out when it was time to listen to my students read about their mothers, sitting at Formica tables and oak tables, peeling potatoes, waiting for the iceman who carried heavy blocks of ice up steps seventy years ago, but I couldn't stop thinking of Thomas's hands on my breasts.

When I got home, I had an hour before the kids would be back from school. Thomas's truck was gone, and there were three messages from him on the machine. They all said, "This is your neighbor. Where are you?"

When I called his house there was no answer, and I could not help myself, I stopped for milk at the Grand Union, then drove up to the Hill.

There were only three vehicles in the parking lot, including Thomas's truck. Losing yourself in the eighteenth century could have been what Americans craved after the great towers of the twentieth century had been destroyed, but they wouldn't admit it. The Hill looked like it might have when Thomas Jefferson visited it, if you squinted and didn't look at the cars.

I hurried out of the car and went looking for Thomas. It was a hot day, a big sunny summer day at the beginning of September, when the sky looked innocent. You couldn't see them, but you could hear the buzz of the air force planes zipping overhead.

I pushed open the front door, the way people have for three hundred years. The front hall was empty; the cabinets of fossils and chairs with velvet ropes across their arms were still. I headed to the gift shop for a ticket, but the gift shop was locked. I continued, illegally, through the big house, down the narrow stairs to the kitchen, where I had encountered Robin and her butter churn. The churn was there, but it was still and Robin was not in sight.

I put my hands on the wooden churn and pushed up and down. There was cream in there, and I thumped it up and down a few times.

I was doing this, in my modern garb, when Thomas walked in. He was dressed the part, in his muslin clothes, with the collar tied loosely with leather string. His chest was strong, with a few curls of white hair.

We stared at each other. He looked like he was going to walk up the stairs, but he came behind me like he did in my kitchen and put his arms around me, placing his hand on the wooden stick.

"This is the dasher," he said.

I didn't say a word.

He churned the cream, which did not, in fact, smell

sour at all. The room got hotter, as he churned and churned. I felt dizzy hot, with his body so close to me.

And then he was touching, not with his hands, but with his body, pressed up hard against mine.

The door was not locked. He hands were off the dasher, and he unscrewed the lid to the churn. He lifted off the top with one hand, and with the other reached down and stuck his fingers in the sweet butter. He put his fingers to my lips. I was licking the butter and his fingers when we heard footsteps on the stairs. Thomas quickly wiped his hands on his muslin pants and pulled away from me.

"Are you okay?" he whispered, as a scraggly band of tourists entered the room.

I stood at the churn, my hands now on the dasher. Thomas started talking about butter as if he knew what he was talking about.

"The correct word is *clabber*, when the cream turns to butter," he said.

"After you've made caraway seed bread, you can always add a dollop of fresh butter," he said, as he grabbed a wooden spoon from the spoon rack.

He walked over to the churn and ladled out a fresh scoop for the tourists to admire.

I stood poised at the churn with my modern-day clothes, with the taste of fresh butter still on my tongue, hoping they would think I was a statue.

A small child, who should have been in school as far as I was concerned, tugged on my leg and said, "I think this is a stupid place," which made me miss Pete.

When Thomas and I were able to flee, the sunlight veiled the fields behind the manor. The planes were still buzzing overhead, so I held my hands to my ears. Thomas grabbed me by the waist and we ran that way, far out into the pasture, past the cows.

"Lie down," he said and I did.

We lay down in the field, hugging and hugging and rolling around. He was kissing my face so tenderly I started crying, and my hair was matted against my cheeks in the tears. There was unbuttoning and un-buttoning and he was touching my breasts again, so I wanted to scream, and those muslin pants just slipped off and he was inside me. The cows began mooing at the same time I cried out, and Thomas collapsed on top of me.

Neither of us talked for a long time, and then Thomas whispered in my ear, "Sweet and crazy."

"What?" I said.

"My parents were both deaf. Once my mother said we were having meat and gravy for dinner, and my father said, 'Sweet and crazy? Sweet and crazy?' "

"You're sweet and crazy," I said.

"Is that little boy going to live with you?" he said, gently kissing my ear.

I shrugged, not thinking about Omar now. I was thinking, I'd slept with my neighbor, a widow woman with a colonial man outside in the fields. I was thinking, the cows knew our secret.

"Who was that young woman at your house?" I whispered.

Thomas shut his eyes. "I'm not sure. She might be a relative. I have a big family. She left a note that says she's going to visit on the fifteenth."

Walking back to my car, after we'd kissed some more in the cooper's shed, I picked pieces of grass off my damp legs and arms.

Thomas went diligently to his cooper's shed while I staggered to the parking lot. When I got to my car, I examined myself in the rearview mirror. I removed a stick of straw from my hair, and tried to pat the flush from my cheeks. I raced home, and a quarter mile before our house, at the pond, I found myself behind the school bus. I couldn't pass it, so I clutched the steering wheel and swore instead. I wanted to go home and take a shower before I greeted Pete and Omar. I waited like a virtuous woman as the bus slowly pulled up to each house and the big Stop sign on the side of the bus swung open.

When the bus reached our house, I parked behind it and ran out with the bag of milk. I hurried to catch up with the boys as they banged up the steps with their backpacks, but they ran past me, not knowing how my life had changed.

The only greeting I received was when Pete yelled, "Your hair looks funny."

I waved to the bus driver, then turned around and hurried into the house. I was famished. We all headed for the kitchen, where I poured myself a big bowl of

Rice Krispies and milk and stood in front of the defrosted refrigerator wolfing it down. Pete grabbed two small bags of chocolate-chip cookies from the bowl on the table.

"We're going under the porch for our club," he said, pulling Omar by the sleeve, and they were gone.

It was hot on September 12, summer hot. I have an air conditioner in my bedroom, the mommy-daddy bedroom as Pete calls it. The other rooms just have fans, except Pete's, which somehow has a little breeze on its own. I began by scrubbing the counters. When Ed died, along with the casseroles and pies, people delivered groceries to our door, bags and bags of hot dog buns, six jars of strawberry jam, eight jars of homemade tomato sauce, sacks of Idaho potatoes, large bags of pasta in every different shape, strings of dried apricots. The fact was, my kitchen had food for the rest of our given lives.

I put a large pot of water on to boil. I was going to make pasta and sauce, wagon wheels for the boys, and corn muffins. Ed always liked corn muffins. The phone rang while I was stirring eggs into the cornmeal.

"What are you doing?" said Thomas.

"I'm cooking."

"I didn't know you cooked."

"My child eats, of course I cook," I said, and then I dropped the phone into the batter. I was wiping it off, yelling into it, but a moment later, Thomas was in the kitchen with me.

"I have steak," he said, holding out a raw steak in his bare hands. "Do you make steak?"

"I'm not so good at that," I said, holding the dripping phone over the sink.

"I'll do it," he said. "Barbecue."

A half hour later I was setting the picnic table in our backyard with Rugrats birthday party paper plates. Thomas was grilling in his yard, his head bent in concentration, still wearing his muslin clothes. Pete and Omar were carrying buckets of sand and dumping them in the middle of the grass.

Pete ran over to the picnic table. "Is Omar going to live here?"

"For now," I mumbled. "How's school?"

"When there's a hundred days of school we're having a party. We have homework. We have to write three *A* words."

"What's an *A* word?" I said, anchoring the paper plates with cups of lemonade.

"*A* is for airplanes that crashed into the control towers," said Pete. "And apple and I don't know what else."

He ran back to Omar and I wandered over to Thomas at the grill.

"Do you like to cook out?" I said.

"I don't have a stove," he replied.

"Yours broke?"

"There wasn't one when I moved in."

It was true. Four or five times on winter evenings,

Ed had pulled me to the kitchen window and pointed out to see Thomas, in a coat, with a Davy Crockett hat, grilling in the dark, holding a flashlight and spatula.

"Why don't you get a stove?"

"I have a toaster oven. I have a coffeemaker."

I nodded. "Was your wife a good cook?"

"She cooked."

I went back over to the picnic table.

Dusk came slowly, and the boys kept carrying their buckets of sand. I wondered if someone drove by, and saw this man grilling in his muslin clothes in one yard, and me trying to bat down the paper plates in the adjacent yard, would the driver of the car know we had lain down in the field together.

Omar burst into tears, and Pete came running to me.

"I didn't push him or anything," Pete said. "He asked where my daddy was and I told him he's dead and he pushed me. That's why I pushed him."

I ran to Omar and knelt down and put my arms around him and Pete stood with his face down, playing with my hair.

"I want my mommy's 'cation to be over right now," said Omar.

"I do too," I mumbled. "Your father will call soon."

"Steak's almost ready," called Thomas, picking up the meat with a large fork.

Finally we all sat down, the boys on one side of the picnic table. Thomas and me on the other. I cut Omar's meat and Thomas cut Pete's meat, and we ate silently.

"We should have salad," said Thomas. "Next time we'll have salad."

"So the girl's coming back in two days?" I said.

Pete had left the table now and was pulling on Omar's arm, but Omar was politely sitting with the grown-ups.

"Would you like to be excused, Omar?" I said.

"Yes, please, thank you for dinner. Am I going home now?"

"Maybe you'll sleep here another night, okay?"

"But then I want my mommy," said Omar.

"Okay, go play," I said.

Thomas and I sat side by side, and I was pushing the wagon wheels around with my fork. "You're a good cook," I said.

"Did the girl in the Mustang talk?" said Thomas. "Did she use sign language or anything?"

"She talked. She definitely could hear."

"My parents came from Scotland, but they met in Tennessee. My father had a younger brother who was deaf also. They had to leave him behind. When my father was a boy, he sneaked out of town one night in a wagon covered with hay. When he peeked out he could see his little brother running after the wagon, silently screaming his name. I grew up around a lot of deaf people. It's an emotional subject with me."

"I'm sorry," I said.

Thomas shrugged. "Would you like any more?"

I shook my head, and that was the end of our dinner party.

• • •

The weekend arrived and Saturday, September 15, arrived, but nobody else did. I had washed the kitchen floor and even stacked Ed's shoes in the back of my closet in somewhat of a neat pile. Omar was still with us. Mazur called every night, and I looked forward to his calls. He talked in a soft voice, not crying, but with tears around the edges of his words. He had gotten the whole story. His wife's brother worked in the South Tower. She was in the subway on the way to visit him, studying her New York City guidebook. When she arrived at Chambers Street, she headed up the steps, guidebook in hand. She emerged onto the street just as the South Tower began to collapse. That's when she got caught up in the stampede. She tripped on debris. Someone fell on her and she broke her leg.

Mazur talked softly about his wife, but in one of the calls he told me about how when he was a little boy in India he used to listen to the Tour-de-France on the radio. "I only had sisters, but I had make-believe bicycle brothers and we used to train for the Tour-de-France."

Mazur called on Sunday morning. "She'll be okay. I'm coming home," he said wearily. "She is tired, very tired. She wants to stay with her brother's wife for a while. She will be on crutches. I'll be back with the baby tomorrow. Do you know any baby-sitters?"

"I don't," I said. "The baby can stay here while you get someone."

When I hung up I looked at the boys out the kitchen window. His wife was alive. I was envious. The kids were lying on top of each other, wrestling in a messy heap. The last thing I needed was a baby around.

At midnight when the boys were sleeping head to foot in Pete's bed, the cat curled on top of the TV with the sound turned off, as CNN replayed and replayed the towers crashing mutely.

Thomas walked in silently and sat next to me on the couch. We held hands there, first gripping tightly to watch the horror, and then he was stroking my palms with his cooper fingers. He pulled me up off the couch and led me out the kitchen door. There were stars out, thousands twinkling in the clear sky. It was quiet. The air force jets were gone to some secret place.

We were standing by the picnic table, and you could see from the kitchen light that it was cleared, just one Rugrats paper plate in the corner. We were looking up at the stars, holding hands, and then very slowly Thomas turned me around to face him and bent me back over the picnic table.

We were like that together, where hours before we had our innocent meal. We were like that afterward, him lying on top of me, stroking my hair.

When he climbed off of me, he kissed my forehead.

"Do you want to come sleep?" he said, softly.

"I think I'll stay out here for a while," I said, turning my head. "You go home. I'll see you in the morning."

I stayed lying on the table in a haze. When I was

five years old, my father's sister came to stay with us, and I remember nothing about her but her mint mouthwash and that in the middle of dinner she raised her glass and said, "Men drift and disappoint. Either they die or leave or stop talking."

I thought about my boy, and Omar, and wondered what kind of men they would be. And I thought about Thomas. I had never made love with my husband on the picnic table or the kitchen table or any table for that matter. I peeled myself off the table. I went inside and took a hot shower. I was more relaxed than I'd felt since I learned to float on my back in the YMCA pool when I was seven.

My older students never wrote brazenly about sex. One woman, Beatrice, who was eighty-five and raised in Louisiana, wrote, "I loved to take naps with my husband while my kids were over at a friend's house. Sometimes we took a nap, and then we napped again." When she read that aloud she winked.

After my shower, I slept for five hours.

In the morning I woke without an alarm and as I packed up the boys for kindergarten, they screamed, "Apple, airplane, and ape!"

Thomas came up the steps carrying a cup of coffee.

"How are you?" he said.

"Fine thank you," I whispered back. "We have to get to school now."

Just then Mazur drove up and slowly, slowly got out of his car, and opened the back door to get the baby boy from the car seat. Thomas and I were standing on the porch, while the boys scrambled around like squirrels.

Mazur solemnly marched up the steps, clutching the baby.

"I'm so sorry about your brother-in-law," I said. "I'm glad your wife's okay." I reached for the sweet giggling baby with dark hair. As I reached, Mazur put out his arms so we hugged with the baby between us.

"Hi baby," I said. "Hi baby boy. What's his name?"

"Henry," said Mazur. "My wife wanted him to have an American name. She'll be okay. She's just tired, very tired. She loved her brother very much. I did, too. We played cricket together."

Thomas put out his hand now to Mazur. "Hello," he said. "I'm very sorry about your loss. I'm glad your wife is alright."

"I don't know how to tell Omar. He loved his uncle."

The boys burst around the corner of the house. "Kindergarten babies, stick our head in gravy, wash it out with bubble gum, now we're in the navy!"

They jumped on the steps, not saying hello to anybody.

"I'll take them to school," I said. "You must be exhausted."

Mazur tried to reach for Omar, but he pulled away.

"Where's Mommy?" he said.

Mazur shook his head, "She's going to visit in New York a little longer."

The boys ran down the steps and Mazur said, "My sister is back at the house. She'll watch the baby," taking the baby back from my arms. "I'll pick up Omar later."

I herded Pete and Omar into my car, and drove off as Mazur stood on the porch holding his baby, next to Thomas. I had the distinct sensation I was sailing wildly on high seas.

I always ask my students to write about love. My student Lucille, from Russia, once wrote: "You know what love is? My own grandfather back in Russia. In summer we were playing with him out under the trees. He told me to go in and tell my grandmother there was a man out in the yard who wanted to see her. I ran in and told my grandmother. She wiped her hands on her apron and then she smoothed her hair. Of course it was my grandfather. He was the man who wanted to see her, day after day after day."

I dropped the kids at school and raced to the YMCA. As the air force bombers raced overhead, I needed someone to tell me a story.

I gave my students the assignment of "a memory of food" to write about in class. I sat staring out the window at the innocent September parking lot, watching two plastic bags playing tag in the wind, as they wrote.

I liked that my students were old enough to be my grandparents. There were fifteen of them, all gray-haired, with their heads bent to their papers on the old attached desks.

After twenty minutes, I said, "One more minute," in my teacher's voice.

I watched the clock, then said, "Now please put down your pens."

Lucille lifted her eyes first. She had curly soft hair and bright green eyes that hid the 3 A.M. anguish of long-gone husbands and children.

"Lucille," I said. "Would you like to start?"

"I grew up in the back of a candy store," she wrote. "My mother was a health nut, so we had to eat whole wheat bread at every meal and only one piece of candy a week. On Thursdays, the rag man came, and he was our treat, because we got to pet his horse *and* he secretly slipped my brother and me each a smooth slab of toffee his wife had made."

I listened to stories about eating chestnuts in a barn as bombs fell in Poland, but I could feel Thomas's hands on my shoulders, and slowly lifting my dress.

I gave my students another assignment so that I could daydream.

"And now a memory of learning to drive," I commanded, and they did.

As they wrote, I tried to piece together a portrait of Thomas. He was my neighbor. He was a cooper. He worked at a colonial restoration and made casks for whiskey. He was divorced. He did not have children. He was often strapping tools and barrels onto the roof of his truck.

The next week the kindergarten was studying the letter *B: Bring in three pictures of things that start with the letter* B. "Breast, bosom, boudoir," I scribbled in my notebook as my students put down their pens.

That afternoon, Pete bounded off the bus alone, without Omar. I was rocking on the porch swing, reading my students' handiwork, as he climbed the steps. "Don't kiss me," he commanded. "If you kiss me, I'll give you a ticket."

I rocked and nodded silently. But then I could not help myself, and I called to him as he went in and slammed the screen door. "How was school?"

I felt like an exchange student. In high school there were always one or two kids in junior year who went away to foreign lands who came back to Ash Creek changed, and they were referred to from then on as "exchange students." Their haircuts were different, and so was their walk, but it was something else. They had had secret adventures that had changed them forever. Ed's dying had that effect on me.

Pete came out on the porch eating one Hostess Twinkie and clutching another.

"I need two," he said, as I started to protest.

"Fine," I said. "How's Omar?"

"His daddy picked him up. Why don't you marry us a new daddy?"

He sat next to me and we swung.

"I can't just get one at the store. There's no daddy store," I said.

"Well, get one when I'm at school," he said, and then he jumped off the porch swing. "And get one that doesn't yell."

"Daddy yelled sometimes," I said. "Remember when you pulled all his books off the shelf, or when you used to shove the books in the bookcase really far?"

"I don't remember," he called, running down into the yard as Thomas drove up in his truck.

Pete grabbed Thomas's hand and they walked up the walk and onto our porch together.

Thomas was fuming. "Those goddamn Arabs. Do you realize they paid cash for their first-class tickets? This country is so damn naive."

Pete jumped on my lap. "Thomas said 'goddamn.' Thomas said 'goddamn.' "

"Please watch what you say," I murmured to Thomas, but Thomas was on a rant.

"They should send them all back," he fumed.

"How can you say that?" I protested.

"We trained these guys how to fly!" shouted Thomas.

"Don't scream at my mother!" said Pete.

"Well thank you, Pete," I said, rubbing his back. "Thank you very much."

"Will you play Candy Land with me?" Pete said, pulling on Thomas's arm.

"You get the game, I'll play," he said.

"No, at your house," said Pete.

"In a little bit. I'm talking to your mother."

"You're yelling at my mother."

Pete stomped inside to get the game, while Thomas continued with his lecture. His voice was lower, but his tone was furious. "We trained these goddamn guys?"

"I know, I know," I murmured. "I wonder how Omar's doing. What a way to start kindergarten . . ."

Pete came back on the porch clutching the Candy Land game.

"Bomb. Butt. Bellybutton," he said. "We have to bring in three *B* words."

Thomas and Pete went next door.

As soon they did, the phone rang. It was my friend Joya. She was in her car, talking on the cell phone, and would arrive any minute. I could not dissuade her.

Ten minutes later, Joya was in my kitchen at the table. Joya is one of those flat-chested women who never wears a bra, but you're always very conscious of her breasts. She is five ten, has dark hair, wears sandals practically all year, and has a toe ring. She was wearing a purple T-shirt and jeans. A masseuse, she sat at the table massaging her right hand with her left.

"This thing is making my kids crazy," she said. Her children were eight and eleven, two girls. "They say they never ever want to go on an airplane, not that we ever do, anyway . . ."

"Would you like some coffee?" I said. "Sorry, herbal tea? Would you like tea?"

She shook her head and kept massaging her hand. "So how are you?" she said. "Your skin looks good."

"My skin?" I blushed.

"Yes, you having sex? Those endorphins make your skin good."

"Joya! Are you having sex? Of course you are, you always are." I rustled around at the stove, putting on water, even though I wanted neither tea nor coffee. I could see Thomas now in his backyard, and he tipped his baseball hat. I put up my hand and gave a quick wave.

"Who are you waving to?" snapped Joya.

"My neighbor," I said, clearing my throat.

"That's who you're having sex with?"

"You should be a psychic, not a masseuse."

"I am. I'm getting into that more. Your neighbor? Isn't that dangerous?"

She leaped up from the kitchen table.

"No," I pushed her away from the window. "Don't look."

We both ducked down.

We were squatting like ducks by the counter under the sink, when Thomas walked in.

"We're looking for my contact," said Joya, standing up. "Hello," she said, putting out her massaged hand. "I'm Joya."

"Hello. Thomas," said Thomas. "Did you find it?"

"Where's Pete?" I said.

"He's looking for moths at my house."

"This is very cozy," said Joya.

Joya said, "Well, I just dropped by. I have a client in fifteen minutes. If you know anybody who needs a massage, here's my card," she said, handing Thomas a card.

I hate jealousy. I was a widow. I wasn't supposed to be jealous.

"Thank you," said Thomas. "I feel in pretty good shape," he said, looking at me.

"You can stay," I said to Joya. "Would you like some coffee?" I asked Thomas, but he was at the coffee-maker, making some on his own.

Joya gave me a thumbs-up sign behind his back. "Nice meeting you, neighbor," she said. "I'll be calling you, Hanna," she said.

"Hope you find your contact," called Thomas.

As soon as she left, Thomas and I were hand in hand, walking around the house like we were on a garden stroll. Pete came running in, and we all ended up in Pete's room. There were piles of clothes and toys all over the floor, probably only decipherable from above, like the mysterious mounds of an ancient Indian burial ground.

We sat down on the floor. Pete plopped down on Thomas's lap.

"You smell funny," said Pete.

In fact he did smell of bayberry and ginger.

"Olden-day smells," said Thomas.

"Did you live in the olden days?" said Pete. He was setting up the Candy Land board now.

Thomas said, "No, but my parents had hearing aids the size of a cigarette pack. Neither of them could ever hear me, and they forbade me to use sign language."

"Cigarettes make your lungs black," said Pete, stacking the little cards of colors and desserts.

"Do you know sign language?" I said.

"One of my cousins, who is also deaf, taught me when I was Pete's age. The girl in the Mustang might be one of his kids."

We played Candy Land as if that were the normal thing to do. For a moment, none of us talked, and I thought of Orville and Wilbur. In 1912, Wilbur wrote, "From the time we were little children my brother Orville and myself lived together, played together, worked together and, in fact, thought together," and I wanted another baby for Pete.

The phone rang and Pete jumped up to get it. I could hear him announce "ThisisPetewhoisthisplease?" into the phone.

He came running back, holding out the phone to me. "It's Omar's daddy."

I took the phone, and felt myself blush. Thomas raised his eyebrows.

"Yes," I said. "Bring them over."

When I hung up I said, "Instant baby."

"What's instant baby?" said Pete.

"Mazur's bringing over Omar and his little brother, Henry, for us to watch for a few hours, not sleep over."

Pete leaped into the air and the Candy Land game scattered.

Thomas stood up. "I'll see you," he said. "I'm going to be gone for a few days."

I tried not to look startled.

"Oh," I said. "Tonight? Where are you going?"

"I have a job."

"You sound like a criminal."

"Barrels. I make barrels for bourbon, you know that."

When Mazur drove up, Thomas was at his house, but his truck was still out front. Mazur rang the front bell. I smoothed my hair before I answered it.

"I can't stay," he said, handing me fat Henry. "Thank you. Thank you very much."

Henry latched onto me like an octopus with his chubby hands. His father bent down to kiss his head.

"Good-bye," I waved from the porch, and I put up Henry's hand to wave as well.

The boys were at the kitchen table eating macaroni and cheese and I was holding baby Henry on my hip, when Joya called. I could barely hear her because Pete shouted, "Knock, knock," and Omar said, "Who's there?"

"Pete."

"Pete who?"

"Pizza pie is good for you."

I cradled the phone under my ear and snuggled Henry.

"The neighbor's cute," said Joya. "What's with the clothes?"

"Muslin. He works up at the Hill. He's a cooper."

"What does that mean?" said Joya. "He's cooped up? A hermit?"

"He makes wooden barrels, wooden things."

"Wooden things. That's handy," said Joya. "Kids?"

"No. Divorced."

"Neighbors could be dangerous, but enjoy it."

"Thank you," I said, as Henry tried to grab the phone.

Thomas walked in swinging the keys to his truck. Baby Henry started crying, and I handed him to Thomas.

"I have to go," I hissed to Joya.

"Neighbor?" she said.

"Definitely the psychic thing," I said. "Good-bye."

"Who was that?" said Thomas.

"A friend," I said.

"The one who was here?"

"What's sidekick?" said Pete.

"You," I said. "You're my sidekick."

The boys were kicking each other under the table.

"Omar wants to be a tooth fairy when he grows up," said Pete. "Can he?"

"I have to go," said Thomas, handing baby Henry back to me.

I walked outside with Thomas.

"Drive carefully," I said, into his mouth, as we kissed, and then he kissed baby Henry.

"Like a demon," he said.

Thomas drove off fast, and flashed his lights on and off. When I returned to the kitchen, Omar was sitting politely at the table eating his macaroni and cheese, with his napkin tucked into his shirt.

Pete was standing on his chair and announced, "I want to go to the islands of the Bahamas."

I heard Mazur drive up at precisely eight o'clock, while I was sitting on the couch watching CNN and the horror. The baby was sleeping next to me as I stroked his baby ears.

I flicked off the TV just as Mazur knocked on the front door. I put one hand to my lips and waved him in. He came in and stood very close to me. He smelled vaguely of the dry cleaner store, and his olive skin and narrow waist and pressed shirt made me dizzy.

He said quietly, "Can you believe your husband is gone?"

"Sometimes not. Sometimes I can't believe any of it, but we had time to say good-bye."

The boys came running in and baby Henry woke up and almost rolled off the couch. Mazur and I both caught him in time, and Mazur scooped up his son.

"We have to go, Omar," he said.

"Why can't we have a sleepover?" said Pete.

"Sleepover! Sleepover! Sleepover!" the boys chanted.

"It's a school night. Some other time, soon," I said.

Mazur and I said nervous good-byes, and he took baby Henry and Omar home. Pete fell sound asleep on the couch. I must have, too, for about an hour, but then I had the sense to wake up and carry him into bed. My son will be five in two weeks, October 1, a birthday without his father for the first time. Other years I complained because Ed never cared what I put in the party bags. I would like to think I would not complain about anything if he rose from the dead.

I stood at the stove looking out at the dark, empty yard. I had to send out invitations for a pizza-and-chocolate-cake party for Pete. We would do it in the backyard. Sack races, three-legged races, Simon Says. We could hang little doughnuts from the trees on strings, and see if they could catch them in their mouths while their hands were tied behind their backs. Pin the tail on the donkey. Kids still liked that.

I made up a list of fourteen children, from school, camp, and the neighborhood, including Pete and Omar. We would have it Saturday, September 29, at 3 P.M.

Thursdays I worked full days at the library, and I always liked those days, cocooned by facts that nobody needed anymore. Thursday, September 20, I sat at the reference desk, in front of the computer. When nobody needed attention, I wrote the birthday invitations on fire truck–shaped cards I'd bought at the ninety-nine-cent store one day when Ed was still alive. Aeons passed. Whole universes were created. Seven hundred million years ago flatworms and jellyfish ruled the earth. Thirty-five million years ago the first dog barked. Three hundred and sixty thousand years ago man or woman first controlled the use of fire. And here I was planning a party to celebrate five years of this one crazy child's life on earth, who was up to letter C in class. Cat. Candy. Crash.

That evening, when Pete was under the front porch playing "tower crash" with a little boy from down the street, the girl in the blue Mustang pulled up in front of the house. She sat there with the motor running, and I sat on the porch, frozen like I was playing freeze tag. Then she turned the motor off and just sat in the car.

I got up slowly and made my way to her car. She was wearing a halter top again, a different one, with flowers, and short shorts. Her long blonde hair was back in a ponytail. Both hands were on the wheel, as if she were still driving, and she held an unlit cigarette between her lips.

"Can I help you?" I said.

She took the cigarette out of her mouth. "I'm having some," she sighed, "trouble. I have to talk to Thomas."

For some reason, before I answered her or said, "What kind of trouble?" I tried to figure out whether I should bring in pretzels or goldfish for kindergarten snack the next day, and apple juice or Hawaiian Punch.

"What kind of trouble?" I finally asked. "Do you want to get out?" I said, even though I had no desire for her to do so.

She shook her head and finally turned toward me. She was very pretty, with perfect skin and sharp blue eyes, even with all that smoking.

Pete bolted out from under the porch with blood all over his mouth. He didn't say anything, just ran and threw his arms around me and rubbed the blood all over my shirt.

"What is it? What happened?" I tried to pull away so I could get a look at his face. "Did you get hurt? What?"

He mumbled something I couldn't hear.

"What?" I repeated.

"I said I got a bloody nose!" he whispered and ran into the house.

He always got bloody noses. He just did. I'd taken him to the doctor about it and he wasn't a hemophiliac or anything, and by now he knew how to stop it with a wet washcloth himself.

I hurried after him, and turned back to yell, "Sorry!" to the girl, but she was revving the engine, and by the time I got to the door, she had sped off.

Pete was slumped on the couch in front of the TV with a washcloth in front of his face, watching the Cartoon Channel. I went to touch his head, but he jerked away.

"How do you know they're not going to crash into the control towers again? I'm never going on an airplane."

"Twin towers," I said quietly. "They'll try and make it extra safe now."

"Well, what if the bad guys dress up as good guys?"

I went into the bathroom, pulled off my shirt, and tried to scrub out the blood.

"They'll have extra people on the planes to make sure they're no bad guys," I called over the running water.

I still needed new bras. I looked at my breasts and lifted them up with my wet hands.

I wrung out my T-shirt and hung it over the shower rod, then pulled on my robe.

I walked back into the living room and said to Pete, "It won't happen again. They're going to make the planes extra safe. Is it still bleeding?"

Pete threw the bloody washcloth on the floor. The nosebleed had stopped. "Of course it's going to happen again," he said. "I want a bigger family."

"We have a big enough family," I said meekly.

"No, we don't. We have three, Mimo, me, and you."

"You're right, I've always wanted a big family," I admitted.

"So get one, you're a grown-up."

The next day, on the way home from work, I stopped at Personally Yours, the underwear and bathing suit store in town. The woman who ran the place, Penny Holton, was considered to be a prostitute, although there was no evidence that anybody slept with her. She was in her sixties, with curly dyed red hair, and always wore tight-fitting body suits and gold chain belts and high, high heels. She lived above the store.

When I walked in, she was reading a movie magazine on the glass counter. She let her half-glasses drop from the gold chain onto her big breasts. She was also said to have implants. I always liked her. She had one daughter who left town as soon as she could and became a lawyer.

What I needed to do was throw away all my old underwear with threads hanging off, and get sexy bras and underpants. I could not bring myself to say the word *panties* out loud, and the term *thong* made me short of breath.

I had the strong sense that Penny Holton could see through my clothes.

She did not say hello. Instead she said, "Thirty-two C?"

I did not say hello back. I just nodded meekly.

She turned and took two plastic drawers out of the cabinet behind her, and began laying out bras in plastic covers like she was going to play a game of solitaire.

"White, cream, black, plain, lacy, quilted, strapless . . . pick your flavor," she said. And then she added, "It's not easy being single in this town."

"Cream," I said, "with straps, something plain, I

mean not plain, pretty, but not fancy. I don't go out much."

She held up a plastic bag with a bra and shook out a cream-colored one with lace stitching around the edges.

I did not say, "My neighbor bends me over the picnic table at night."

But Penny Holton knew. I knew she knew. I wanted to pull up one of the high stools at the glass lingerie counter and ask her opinion on life, but I kept my eyes steadily on the bras.

"I'll take two of those," I said. I needed underpants, but I couldn't make myself ask for them. I'd have to order some from a catalog.

"You should try them on," she said. "You'll want a comfortable fit," she said, as if we were talking about sensible shoes.

"No, no, I have to get home for my son," I said. "I won't need a bag."

"Paper, I'll just wrap them in paper," she insisted, pulling pink tissue paper off the roll.

I paid hastily and stuffed the finery into my book bag.

At the door Penny Holton said, "Men are kind to widows."

I nodded and scurried out to the car.

Driving back to the house, I thought of a special double doll I had as a child. It was two dolls in one, stuck feet to feet, and at each end was a head. You could pull the reversible skirt over one body and then the other, depending on whether you wanted the doll with the blonde hair in a bun with a red dress or the one with the curly brown hair in a nightgown. The doll couldn't sit down, though, so it was always lying on the shelf confused.

I drove in the driveway and a moment later, Pete's bus pulled up. He ran to the house ahead of me, as I was heading up the steps clutching my books and bras.

"How was school?" I hissed.

"I need to breathe on trees so they can get oxygen," he said.

The next days I was abuzz with birthday plans, as much as one woman can be abuzz. Pete had two interests in the party. He requested that he have a chocolate cake with chocolate frosting, with plastic motorcycles as decor. He also insisted on filling the party bags. There was no theme to this birthday party, but we had spent longer than I would have liked at the ninety-nine-cents store, selecting glow-in-the-dark yo-yos, candy necklaces, some plastic dinosaurs, and sheets of swamp animal stickers. When we got home, Pete meticulously lined up each group of gems and filled the gaudy little bags.

Several nights before Pete's birthday, I was at the kitchen table, making a list of party games at 1:30 A.M., wearing one of my new bras and one of Ed's old shirts, and fairly presentable flowered underwear, when Mazur called.

"Do you cry often?" he said.

"In the car," I said. "I used to in the shower," but I blushed when I said *shower*, and quickly said, "mainly in the car now. Will your wife be back soon? Pete's birthday is next Saturday, in the backyard if the weather keeps. Would you like to come?"

"Yes, thank you. She doesn't know when she's coming back. Her voice sounds different."

Five minutes after he called, I was standing, bent over with my head on the kitchen counter, when Thomas called.

"Where are you?" I said.

"Tennessee. Are you alright?"

"That Mustang girl is in trouble," I said.

"I know. She's my niece. She's here," said Thomas. "I'll see you when I get back."

"I'm planning Pete's birthday party."

"Am I invited?" Thomas whispered.

"I'd like you to help. I need to attach the pin-the-tail-on-the-donkey thing on the tree, and you could run the sack race. It's Saturday."

"I'll be back tomorrow."

I could hear a teenage girl's voice now in the background, singing, "We all live in a yellow submarine, yellow submarine."

"Well, she can come to the party too."

"Thanks," he said. "Kiss Pete for me."

When we hung up I recalled when my husband forgot my name. He was slowly dying, sleeping with one comforter and two wool blankets, even though it was

July, and I'd gone to bring him some lemonade. He kept asking for lemonade for days, nothing else, and he reached out his hand that was very pale and rubbed my arm. "What's your name?" he murmured.

"I'm Hanna," I said, "your wife," and began to cry.

Saturday, September 29, was a fine outdoor birthday party day. I got up at daybreak, did twenty sit-ups, and then went in to check on the birthday boy. Pete looked like a little king, lying on his back, with his hands behind his head.

I sat on his bed, saying the party list over and over in my head. Omar, Jimminy Cricket, as the kids called him—the little boy from down the street, who did have a strange voice—Kevin McMahon, Nancy Bueti, four other children from school who had said yes, and then Joya said she would come with her kids, and Thomas and his niece, if they showed up. That was the list I had.

Pete opened his eyes. "It's a drop-off party, right?" he said.

"Happy birthday, Mr. five-year-old."

"Is it a drop-off?" he said.

I rubbed his hair. "If they want to drop them off they can, but some parents may stay."

"It's a drop-off party," said Pete, rubbing his eyes. "Five-year-olds have drop-offs."

"Technically yes. What do you want for breakfast?"

"Cake. What's technically?"

"You can't have the cake until the party. Technically is officially."

"I don't want fish."

"Pete, I'll be in the kitchen, when you're ready to get up. I left frosting in the bowl. You can have that, but not the cake."

At noon people began to arrive. The picnic table was set with a Rugrats paper tablecloth and plates and cups, and some heavy rocks to keep the cloth from blowing away. The leaves were red and yellow, the sun was bright, with a slight breeze. I'd tacked up the pin-the-tail-on-the-donkey banner to the side of the house, and strung marshmallows on strings from the maple tree.

Mazur showed up first with Omar, and the boys immediately raced inside. Mazur was wearing a starched yellow button-down shirt, khakis, and a dark brown belt and shoes. He carried a large covered dish as he walked toward me from the car. The aroma of curry filled the October air.

There was an elegance about Mazur not seen in Ash Creek. The Ash Creek men were of three kinds—the ones I'd grown up with, whom I knew as boys, and had thickened around the waist and lost their hair; those who worked at the air force base and had trim bodies and razor-short hair; and a few from outside who had married local girls. Those men always looked lost and frightened at the mall. There was nobody like Mazur.

"My sister made it," he said, almost as an apology, as he placed the dish on the Rugrats table cloth.

"That smells delicious," I said. "It's so kind of you."

"I'm going to be going to New York again. There are all kinds of papers they need help with." His voice trailed off and he looked up at the sky. "There was a note in someone's coat pocket when they left it to be cleaned. 'Leave town Arabs . . .' "

"I'm so sorry," I said. "Americans aren't great at geography . . ."

Just then Joya drove up, and she and her kids spilled out of the car.

She was wearing the tiniest tank top, no bra, and jeans. She carried a large box wrapped with Rugrats wrapping paper, but managed to massage her hands just the same.

"It's a theme," she said, gesturing at the tablecloth. "Oh hi," she said, reaching out her hand to Mazur. "I'm very sorry to hear about your brother? Brother-in-law?"

"Yes, thank you," Mazur sighed.

Joya handed him a massage card. He looked a bit stunned when he read it, but put it in his pocket.

I hurried off to reattach the pin-the-tail-on-the-donkey banner that was blowing off the house.

Eventually eight children showed up and I had given up on Thomas. I enlisted Joya to help with the games. She put two fingers in her mouth and whistled to get everybody's attention. Most of them ran over, but Pete ran under the porch. I was teary-eyed without Ed on his birthday and crept under the porch to talk to Pete and hide my tears.

We were both squatting under there with his old tricycle and jars of dried-up worms, as I prayed I'd be able to lure him out for his party.

"I don't plan to go to sleep-away college," he said.

"No, no," I said. "You've just started kindergarten. "You don't have to worry about that."

"I'm not worried," he said. "I'm just not going. I don't want to go away."

"You don't have to." I pulled him onto my lap, and we both fell over in the dirt.

"I want to be a train engineer. Do I have to buy a train or do they give me one?" He wasn't crying now.

I wiped his tears from his dirty face. "They'll give you a train. That's part of the deal. You don't have to buy your own train."

"I give out the party bags," he said, creeping out of the porch.

"Yes, yes," I said, but he had already bolted across the lawn.

I bumped my head getting out from under the porch, and was wiping my grimy face, when I saw Thomas organizing the kids for pin the tail on the donkey like he owned the place.

Joya was standing very close to him, helping tie the bandanna around the kids' eyes. Neither of them saw me crawl out from under the porch. I considered retreating, just skipping the birthday, lying in the dirt under the porch, letting myself wallow in memories of Pete's birth with Ed holding my hand, but opted to sneak into the kitchen to wash my face in the sink.

Mazur was in there, with his back to me, at the kitchen table, with his head in his hands.

I ran the water and washed my face, then rubbed it with a dish towel before he could see that I was crying.

Just then the screen door pulled open and Joya came in.

"Hanna!" she started to shout, but then she saw Mazur and covered her mouth. "You're needed outside," she said quietly to me. "I'll stay," at which point she started massaging Mazur's shoulders.

As I ran out Joya was giving advice on the effects of garlic on stress.

Pin the tail on the donkey was winding down. The kids were chasing one another with their blindfolds on. It was the moment before someone would crash into someone else, or the tree.

I clapped my hands together, "It's time to bob for apples!" I said weakly. "Apples!" I called, but only Thomas looked up. He was trying to separate two boys who were wrestling on the ground with their blindfolds on, but he left them and walked over to me.

"Hi," he said, kissing me on the cheek. "Where are all the parents?" he said.

"It's a drop-off," I said.

"Sounds like a drive-by," he said.

Just then Pete ran over with his nose gushing blood, and wiped his nose on my T-shirt. "This is the stupidest," he sobbed.

I tried to comfort him, but wanted to see what had happened at the tree. Two boys were still wrestling— Omar and a fat boy from their class, named Chester, who looked like he was ten. Chester's mother was born-again and made him wear a tie to school. He was not wearing a tie now, but a sweaty T-shirt and it looked like he was going to suffocate little Omar.

Chester's mother had dropped him off. Thomas was prying the kids apart now, but Chester was yelling at Omar. I hesitated, thinking I should go get Mazur, but not wanting him to have to contend with violence in the backyard. I finally got over to the mess of boys. Thomas had his arm around Omar, and was restraining Chester.

Omar looked like a tiny ghost in his stained khaki pants and ironed shirt.

"Is everybody okay?" I said. "Let's play freeze tag. Does anybody want to play freeze tag?"

Pete pulled on my arm. "I have to whisper something to you."

"How about tag?" I repeated, as Pete kept yanking on me.

"I'm going to scream in your ear," he yelled, "if you don't let me tell you a secret!"

Mazur came out of the house rubbing his eyes, and walked over to us.

"What is the problem? Is there a problem?" he said.

Omar looked down on the ground as Pete jumped up and pulled my ear.

"Stop it!" I shouted. This was not the birthday party I'd planned.

Finally I bent down, and let Pete whisper in my ear. "Chester said Omar's going to go to hell because his uncle crashed into the Control Tower and killed everybody."

I stood up. "Oh my God," I muttered.

"Are you okay Omar?" I said. I knelt down and looked into his eyes, but they looked like little stones.

"I think we'll go home now," said Mazur. "Thank you very much," he said formally and shook my hand.

As they drove off, I held Pete's hand and he screamed, "This is the worst day in the universe."

"C'mon," I sighed, "we have to get back to the party."

As we headed to the backyard, Pete held my hand tight like I was taking him to the dentist. "They'll be gone in an hour," I said.

The scene in the backyard appeared to be in slow motion now. The kid they called "Jimminy Cricket" was wearing the pin-the-tail-on-the-donkey banner around his shoulders like a cape, running back and forth playing tag with himself.

Two other kids were dumping the tub of water with the apples all over the grass.

"I'm going over to Thomas's house," announced Pete.

"You can't. I'll go get the cake," I said. "The cake is a fun thing."

"Only if I can light the candles."

"You can't light the candles. Kids can't play with matches, plus I'm supposed to bring it out to you."

"Joya!" I shouted. She was placing more rocks on the picnic table to keep the Rugrats cloth from blowing off, so that it looked like some kind of shrine.

Thomas was valiantly trying to comfort Chester, who was gagging he was sobbing so much. I thought we should send the child home, but his mother was no-where in sight.

Joya left her rock display and came to get Pete. "Pete," she said, massaging his little shoulders. "Could you help with some rocks?"

Pete pulled away from her. "I don't want rocks on my table."

I fled inside. I took the cake off the top of the re-frigerator and lit the candles, six candles, one for good luck. "Please don't let me die before Pete," I whispered. But that didn't sound good. Either way, if he died before me I couldn't bear it. If he died after me, who would take care of him?

I made my solitary parade back outside. The table-cloth had blown completely off the table now, with the plates and cups littering the lawn. Pete was building a small wall with the rocks Joya had collected.

"Happy birthday!" I screamed, and began singing in a wobbly voice. Thomas came over to me, and then all the kids, so we were standing around Pete in a circle, singing as he continued with his fortress.

The end of Pete's birthday party was a blur. No children were left in our backyard. I can attest to that, and there were no more racial slurs hurled. When Chester's mother drove up, I put my hand on Chester's wide back and looked into his mother's eyes as she sat up high in her black SUV. But when I opened my mouth to say that I would not accept ignorance or religious intolerance at my home, Chester opened the door, scrambled up into the backseat, and I did not say a word.

Instead I waved a coward's wave as they drove off into the September sunlight.

I cursed myself for not speaking up, for not "taking life on tiptoe," as my father would say. It was Pete who muttered, "That kid should get fired from his job."

By the end of the day, Joya finally left with her kids. I trooped in the kitchen door with the final stack of paper plates and wadded-up crepe paper, to find Thomas filling glasses with water and sugar at the sink. Pete was ripping open his presents so that I'd have to write, *Thank you for the great gift* on the thank-you cards, not having a clue what anyone gave.

"In the eighteenth century, this is how kids made rock candy," explained Thomas.

"Maybe everybody died in the olden days 'cause they ate rocks," said Pete.

"That's just the name," said Thomas. "Here, do you have any string?" he said, rummaging around in the counter drawers until he found some. "You put string in the glasses and then the candy grows. It's slow, though."

I slid down onto a kitchen chair and listened to Thomas. "Now you know, Pete," he said, "if you cut an onion and your eyes tear, you just hold a small piece of bread in your mouth."

"What if your eyes tear and you're not cutting onions?" I said.

"Then you just cry your heart out," said Thomas.

Someone was knocking at the door.

"Maybe it's someone who forgot a birthday present."

Thomas stayed at his rock candy experiment. Pete tore open a Bob-the-Builder plastic drill, batteries not included. It sounded like a large cat was scratching at the front screen door. I smoothed my hair with a sticky hand and headed through the living room.

It was the girl again, Thomas's niece. Through the screen she still had that bright blonde hair, and she had more of an angelic look now, even with her tiny pink shirt. I would say she had a plaintive look in her eyes.

I didn't want her to bolt, but I wasn't sure I wanted her inside.

"Would you like to come in?" I said.

Talking through the screen was oddly comfortable, as if we were both at a confessional booth.

Pete came out holding the plastic electric drill like

a gun. Thomas must have found batteries, because the thing was buzzing really loudly.

"Please turn that off," I said.

"You're going to get cancer," Pete said to the girl.

"Pete stop it," I said. "I'm sorry," I said to the girl. "Would you like to come in? I'm sorry, I don't know your name."

"Maureen," she said curtly, and then she basically fell into the house, because as she pushed open the screen door, Pete opened it really fast.

"You're a pain in the neck, kid," Maureen said.

"I'm so sorry. Pete, please say you're sorry to Maureen," I said, as I tried to help her up, but she chose to stay lying on the floor. She wasn't hurt. I could tell that. I was having trouble separating "the weak from the shaft" as my aunt used to say.

"Thomas!" yelled Pete. "There's a crazy smoking lady lying on the floor on my birthday!"

Thomas walked in with a glass of sugar water. "What the hell?" he said, spilling some water on Maureen by mistake.

"Everybody's using the *H* word," said Pete, yanking on Thomas's arm.

"You'll get a time-out."

"He should get a time-out," said the girl standing up.

"Hello, Maureen," said Thomas. "Do you think we could have a civil conversation?"

My aunt told me when I was a teenager, that the way to handle someone you're really jealous of is to "woo" them, that's the term she used, even though you want to kill them.

I felt a jealousy I hadn't felt in years, not jealous in a sexual way, although perhaps envious of her youth. My jealousy had more to do with an envy of having a big family the way Thomas did. I tried to smile and said, "Maureen," trying to make her name comfortable in my mouth. "You're welcome to spend the night."

"She can stay at my house," said Thomas, holding the glass of sugar water toward her like he was offering her a cocktail.

"I'm not tired," she said. "I think I'll just drive around. I can always sleep in my car."

"Are you a grown-up?" asked Pete.

"Her name is Maureen," I said.

"Maureen, are you a grown-up?" asked Pete.

That night Maureen came by late after Pete was asleep. The girl made me nervous, but I offered her cake. Soon we sat at the kitchen table eating big slabs and drinking milk. She built a small Lego fortress on the table in between bites.

"My parents are deaf, too," she said in a tumble of words, "and there's a chance my baby will be born deaf."

"Where's the father of this baby?" I said, fumbling with the Legos myself.

Maureen shrugged.

I had the strange desire to confide in Maureen, to tell her that though my parents weren't deaf, they were so crazy about each other that I felt completely alone.

When I was a young woman, I was not having sex in a car or a motel or on my parents' couch. When I was a young woman, I had a heartsick longing to stay home.

"I literally can't talk to my mother," said Maureen, with a laugh. "She can't hear a damn thing I have to say."

I fell asleep on the couch that night, and when I awoke at 3 A.M., I staggered into the kitchen. Maureen was curled up on the kitchen floor like a waif. I couldn't lift the girl, so I went and got a blanket for her. Then I returned to bed and slept two more hours. I got up early and tiptoed back into the kitchen around Maureen. It's possible she was awake, but she did not budge, even while I stirred the pancake batter.

Pete rose early and came into the kitchen wearing his dinosaur pajamas.

"Good morning, birthday boy," I whispered, pointing to Maureen.

"My birthday was yesterday," he said, not seeing Maureen at first. "How many years until I can drive?" He wound up a plastic robotic dog that walked and barked across the table and crashed to the floor, almost hitting Maureen on the head.

She bolted awake.

"Eleven years," I said. "Would you like some pancakes?" I said to both of them. "Thomas said we could go visit him up at the Hill today, if you want."

Maureen got up slowly and left to go to the bathroom.

"I definitely want to," said Pete. "I don't want any

kind of job where you have to give back money. Why does she sleep on the floor?"

"What do you mean 'give back?' " I said, stirring the pancake batter.

"At stores they give you back money, I don't want to do that. I want to keep the money."

The robotic dog was now yipping on the floor on its back.

"Please turn that off," I said. "They give you change when you pay for something. That's not giving back money really."

"I just don't want to give back money. I'll be a fisherman."

Ten minutes later, Pete was eating pancakes at the table and I realized Maureen had driven away.

On the drive up to the Hill I turned the radio on low, and bent my head to hear it, but it wasn't low enough, because Pete piped up from the backseat, "What's a terrorist?" and I realized his generation would learn how to spell that word just as we learned to spell assassination.

"Someone very bad."

"Was Omar's uncle bad?"

"*No*, not at all. Some bad guys crashed into the World Trade Center and Omar's uncle was killed."

"Chester says he was bad."

"Chester's very wrong."

"Anyway, I want a pig to pick me up at school. We're

doing *D* in school next week. Dumb. Dinosaur. Dead."

"Or dog," I said. "You could bring in a picture of a dog," I said, turning up the long drive to the Hill House. I was trembling in my soul, frightened with the air force base nearby, frightened that Pete's life would never be normal. When Pete was three, he fell off his tricycle. When he came in the house with a bloody face, I asked what happened and he said, "A chicken bit me." That's about how dangerous I wanted his life to be. I wanted to hide in the eighteenth century. There were a dozen cars in the lot. We parked and went in to get tickets at the gift shop.

As I opened the door to the shop, tiny bells chimed and the smell of bayberry candles almost knocked me out.

"What smells?" said Pete. "Is this what olden days smelled like?"

I smiled at the woman in the muslin cap and green dress and white apron as I paid for the tickets.

Pete shook his head when the woman gave me change, and muttered, "No way I'd do that job."

The door was partially open behind the counter, and I could see the blacksmith hunched in front of a small television.

I hurried Pete back outside into the October sunshine. He ran toward the Cooper's Shed like he could read the signs. I followed, feeling out of place in my jeans and T-shirt. Thomas ran inside and slammed the door before I got there.

I stood outside, smoothing my hair with one hand,

and put up my other hand in a fist to knock, when Thomas pulled open the door.

"Are you going to punch me?" he said, grabbing my wrist.

"Should I?" I said.

"Have you seen Maureen?" he said, standing back so I could walk in. The walls were lined with shelves of bowls. Beautiful pine barrels stood in rows under the window.

Pete was standing on a stool, hammering away with a wooden mallet on wooden nails on the workbench.

"Thanks for letting him do that," I said.

"Do you want to join him? It helps," said Thomas, offering me a mallet.

Thomas's cell phone rang. He handed me the mallet, reached under his shirt, and took out his phone that was clipped to his muslin pants.

"Cooper," he said brusquely, as if he were in a newsroom. He opened his eyes wide. "Where are you?" he said. "Are you okay?"

Pete shouted, "I love the olden days!"

Thomas put his hand over the phone and screamed, "Stop hammering and be quiet!"

Pete did, and Thomas spoke softly into the phone. "Are you off the road? Why shouldn't I bother? Where are you? Someone's there?"

Thomas muttered "damn," as he hung up. "She's not even old enough to drive."

"Bradley in my class says, 'damn' and 'smoke,' " said Pete, and he began hammering again.

Thomas said, "Pete, could you do a job for me? Could you fill this bucket with acorns for me? I use them to show the schoolkids."

Thomas grabbed a bucket hanging from the ceiling. "This is really a water bucket, but you can fill it with acorns."

Pete jumped off the stool, grabbed the bucket, ran outside, and slammed the door.

A moment later Pete pushed the door back open and stood there like an urchin. "How many acorns?" he pleaded.

"One hundred," said Thomas. "No, one-hundred-one."

Pete turned and bent to his task, and Thomas put his hands on my shoulders. I was sure he was going to say he was in love with Maureen, but he yanked open a drawer at his workbench and a piece of paper flew out. He picked it up and read it aloud:

No colonist shall be seen eating modern food: burgers, Dipsy Doodles, soda pop, etc.

At all times colonists shall be hosts of the Steenhuise family and shall act in a proper and seemly manner.

Colonists shall always wear proper colonial garb on the premises.

Colonists will use language in keeping with eighteenth-century ways and shall refrain from using foul modern words.

"So what?" I said.

"I've never been really good at modern life, modern relationships, but I feel like I have to take care of this girl." He took up a mallet and began banging a piece of wood. "Pete!" he called.

Pete was diligently picking up acorns and placing them in the bucket like they were delicate pearls.

"That's great! Bring me the bucket and we can finish up another time."

Pete kept bent over to his task until Thomas called, "Now!" and he ran over with the bucket.

Thomas grabbed the bucket and placed it at the shed door. Then he ran off ahead of us to the parking lot. Pete followed after him, muttering, "Why don't those kids pick up their own acorns?"

As I hurried to catch up, I recalled when Ed told me about being "married by the glove." He'd come home from the library an August day before Pete was born. He was waving a book in the air. I was very pregnant sitting on the porch swing, swinging tentatively.

"Hanna, you've got to read this book. It's about a soldier who went off to war and proposed to his beloved by letter. He couldn't be there, so she married his glove, which was held up by somebody else."

Thomas raced ahead of us in his truck out of the parking lot, and turned left at the end of the Hill House drive. He honked and waved as we followed and turned the other way.

"I love honking," said Pete, from the backseat. "If

the bad guys crashed into our school, do you know what I'd do?

"What?" I said, smoothing my eyebrows in the rearview mirror.

"I'd duck," he said.

When we got home there was a shaky message from Mazur on the answering machine. It was so quiet I had to turn up the volume.

"What is it? What is it?" shouted Pete, jumping on my bed. The wood frame of the bed was covered with turquoise dinosaur Band-Aids Pete had stuck there when Ed first got sick.

"Be quiet so I can hear," I said, replaying the tape for the third time.

"I need talking," Mazur said. "I need talking." At least that's what I think he said, but he was very quiet.

"He doesn't sound happy," said Pete, jumping off the bed, and lying underneath it.

"I'm going to call back Omar's father now, so please be quiet," I said, sitting on the bed.

I dialed his number at home, but there was no answer. I left a message to call me.

"Please leave a message after the serious beeps," said Pete from under the bed.

"Series of beeps," I said as I dialed the cleaners, even though it was Sunday.

Mazur answered, as if there were a gun at his head. "Hello," he said evenly. "Hello, who is this please?"

"It's Hanna. What's happening?"

"I've been getting calls," he said. "At home, here,

all day and night. They say awful things. If I take the phone off the hook I lose business."

"Did you call the police?"

"No, I think the people in Ohio don't want us here. In all of America."

"You should tell the police. Do you want me to call them?"

As soon as we hung up the phone rang again. It was Thomas.

"Did she call?" he said.

"No trace," I said.

"Fine. I'm going to Tennessee."

Joya knocked on the kitchen door as I was talking to Thomas. I waved her in, and she immediately walked over to the stove and put on water for tea. She raised her eyebrows, pointed next door, and mouthed the word "Neighbor?"

I nodded my head. She took out two tea bags from her T-shirt pocket and dropped them in cups as I tried to comfort Thomas.

"Good-bye," I said. "Good luck."

"Good luck to you," said Joya as I got off the phone. "What is this, the widow's hot line? Maybe I should tell people I'm a widow. I think that's better than divorcée."

I turned the water on really hard and banged a pot on the counter.

"Sorry," she said.

Joya placed the cups of tea on the table and I sat down and put my nose to the cup.

"Ginseng," she said. "Not that you need it, apparently. The air force base is on high alert. Are you sending Pete to school tomorrow?"

"Yes," I sighed. "The child needs kindergarten. They're supposed to go apple picking this week."

"I don't think the world cares about apple picking at this moment, Hanna."

"Well, I do." I took a gulp of the bitter tea and spit it back into the cup.

"You don't do that when you go on a date, do you?" said Joya.

"I'm dating my son," I said.

"I'm keeping my kids home from school tomorrow," insisted Joya.

"Not me," I said. "Look, I think I need to rest right now. You're welcome to sit here and drink that stuff. I'm going in to lie down."

I was lying on my bed when Joya called to me, "That Bin Laden guy needs sex. That's what this is all about," and then I drifted off to sleep.

OCTOBER

Monday arrived, and Pete ran down the steps to the school bus. Two cups of coffee later, I went off to teach. I did not listen to the radio in the car. That day Pete came home with two notes in his backpack. One said there had been incidents of "taunting and bullying" on the playground since September 11:

> Please teach your children that all Americans are our brothers and sisters.

The other note said that there was an outbreak of lice:

> Please be extra vigilant. Do not let your children share hats or brushes with other children. Please send in two dollars monthly for the school nurse to check your child. Thank you.

That night I made hamburgers, slapping the meat
with my hand, while Pete set up a motorcycle race at
my feet.

"We're learning *E* next," he said. "Elephant. Eraser.
Emergency. And Columbus. Columbus and those boys
finded America. Did you know that?"

"Yes I did," I said as the phone rang.

I picked up the phone and I heard Pete mutter. "I
wish I was one of Columbus's boys."

It was Thomas. "Maureen is in trouble."

"Maureen *is* trouble," I said.

"She's my niece."

"Well, we're your neighbors. When is she going to
have the baby?" I said.

"I don't know," he said.

"Should I get the towels ready?"

I heard him ask Maureen when she was going to
have the baby.

"April," he said.

The hamburgers were smoking now, and I turned
off the burner.

Pete screamed, "Fire, fire!" and climbed up onto the
sink to fill a pot with water. He dumped the water on
the hamburgers before I could stop him. The kitchen
was very smoky.

"I have a little emergency here," I said to Thomas.
"I'll see you when you get back."

I hung up and lifted each hamburger out of the pan
with a slotted spoon, and carefully placed one on a

plate for Pete, and one for me. I had forgotten the rolls—they were burned to a crisp in the toaster oven.

"I like Thomas's hamburgers better," said Pete. "I'll divorce you if you make me eat those."

I dumped the hamburgers and rolls in the garbage and poured us each a bowl of Rice Krispies.

"Let's go eat on the picnic table," I said.

As we sat in the dusk, eating our cereal, Pete said, "We had to practice rolling out the door at school."

"What do you mean 'rolling'?"

"In case the bad guys throw a bomb on us," he said.

"We have to write thank-you cards for your birthday. I'll write them if you sign your name."

"Why did Daddy die when he was only forty-five and Chester has a grandmother who's ninety-three?"

"I don't know," I said, mashing my Rice Krispies with the back of my spoon.

"I know," said Pete. "Sometimes God runs out of numbers."

The Friday before Columbus Day, the earth smelled of smashed apples and chestnuts. A schoolwide assembly was scheduled at 9 A.M. The kindergarteners were supposed to sing about the *Niña,* the *Pinta,* and the *Santa Maria.* Parents were invited, but not obligated to attend. I drove Pete to school because I was obligated to attend. Before Pete fell asleep the night before, he said, "Daddy's dead, so you have to come." I decided to take the whole day off. I didn't teach Fridays, and since September 11, the traffic at the library was eerily slow.

"Omar gets to be one of Columbus's boys. Only graders get to be Columbus's boys. How come he gets to be? Is Omar an Arab person?" Pete said quietly from the backseat, where he was crashing two plastic dinosaurs together.

"Actually he isn't," I said. I patted the stack of Ed's mail on the seat beside me. He definitely got more junk mail since his death.

I dropped Pete at K-122 and headed down the steps to the auditorium. The green walls in the hallways were covered with children's drawings of the World Trade Center towers in flames, and planes crashing into them. If you didn't know, you might think they were sweet giant chimneys, with birds flying past. I pushed open the heavy auditorium door. There were parents down in front, and a hand-painted sign hung above the closed curtain on the stage: Welcome Mothers and Fathers.

I took a seat on the aisle near the back and folded my hands together on my lap. A moment later Mazur walked past me toward the front. He was wearing a perfectly pressed olive khaki suit. He didn't see me as he passed, but I softly called his name and he turned. I wondered if he had pressed his own white shirt that morning. He looked pale.

"Would you like to sit here?" I said, pointing to the seat next to me.

He gave a slight bow, and I stood up to let him pass.

He used aftershave that smelled like lilacs. He sat down, face forward, and put his arm on the armrest so it touched my side.

"Would you like to come to the shop after the performance?" he said.

I felt like the whole school was looking at us. "Yes," I said, not turning toward him. "Yes, I'll go back to the shop."

I never thought of the cleaners as a shop. I liked calling it a shop. I imagined myself being married to Mazur, standing at the counter taking everybody's stained clothes. The auditorium was filling up now with parents. I missed Ed and I missed Thomas. I coughed heavily and Mazur removed his arm.

The principal marched on stage and tapped the microphone. It squealed as he said, "In just a moment . . . in just a moment . . . in just a moment, the children will present their Columbus Day performance."

Then the curtain was raised, and a blur of squirming children stood in red, white, and blue crepe-paper costumes. Mrs. Irwin, the music teacher, came out and gave a curtsy in her high heels and flare-out dress. She raised her baton. The kindergarteners stepped forward and began to sing "The Niña, the Pinta, and the Santa Maria" to the tune of "Hello Dolly." Pete was holding hands with a little girl I'd never seen before.

They sang and sang, songs I'd never heard of about Christopher Columbus, and then three large papier-mâché boats wobbled out, with sneakered feet scurrying beneath.

Mazur leaned toward me. "Omar is one of the boys of Columbus."

Just then a large child, who must have been in fourth grade, stepped out of one boat with a large felt hat and a plume. Four tiny children, including Omar, jumped out of the other boats with fishing poles and started running around. Joya had mentioned something about switching from swords to fishing poles after September 11, and I now understood what she was referring to.

"Your son is very good," I smiled.

"So is yours," he nodded solemnly. "In India I taught mathematics," he said quietly.

I nodded, because I did not know what to say.

The performance lasted about a half hour, just enough to make people late to work.

"It is a long weekend," said Mazur. "In India we have no long weekends."

I nodded. In truth, I despised long weekends, ever since I was a child. I never saw the point. We stood up in the throng of clapping parents.

"Tea?" said Mazur. "I must get back to the shop."

We sneaked out during the second encore of bowing fourth graders, and I could feel people staring at us.

I followed Mazur in my car. He drove in his Spotless Cleaners van as carefully as he was pressing a shirt. I sensed he was crying as he drove ahead of me. I had repaired the binding of a book at the library that said men cried as much as women in the Middle Ages. There were no footnotes, but the author claimed you could stop by the roadside on the way to your castle in the 1500s and see clumps of men weeping into their tunics and tights, grown knights with tears rusting down their chain mail and ornate heavy armor, perhaps even shepherds burying their faces in piles of wool.

The shopping center was half empty, and I was able to pull up right next to Mazur's van in front of his shop, which was next to the pizza parlor and Nellie's Nicknack Nook.

There was a wedding gown hanging in the window of the cleaners with a plastic bag over it. Mazur held open the door for me like we were on a date, and I nodded to a young Indian man with neatly combed hair standing behind the counter.

"My cousin," Mazur said.

I held out my hand over the counter and the man bowed. "This is Mrs. Hanna," he said, pointing to me. "She is a widow."

"I am sorry," the man said.

"Hello. Thank you," I said.

"Please," said Mazur, and I followed him behind the counter. He pulled back a maroon curtain, to reveal a small room. Incense candles were burning on top of a television set on either side of a large photograph of a timid young man in a turquoise silk shirt. There was a red couch with gold pillows against the wall.

I sneezed several times.

"Forgive me," said Mazur. "Please sit down."

"Excuse me," I said, reaching for a Kleenex in my pocket.

I did not sit down. "Your brother-in-law?" I said. "He was very handsome."

"Please have tea," said Mazur. There was a small burner on the counter in the corner, and an ornate enameled teapot was boiling. Two gold cups sat ready to be filled.

It seemed my destiny for people to offer me tea when I was not in the mood.

"Thank you," I said. "Tea is lovely. Thank you very much."

Mazur poured the water gracefully into a mesh strainer full of tea leaves over one cup. As he moved the strainer to the second cup, the crash of a large rock shattered the front window.

Mazur's cousin screamed from behind the counter as Mazur dropped the teapot to the ground. Hot water sprayed all over his pants, and we both ran to the front of the shop.

The whole front window had been smashed. Tiny bits of glass glittered across the floor and counter. The wedding dress was crumpled in its plastic in the corner. Outside in the mall it looked like people were rehearsing a scene from a movie, as they pushed their shopping carts, scurrying toward their cars.

"Dial 911," I said. "Dial 911," but Mazur and his cousin had grabbed brooms and were sweeping up. They were talking Indian in fast, shrill voices to each other.

"Dial 911," I repeated as I reached over to the wall phone behind the counter.

Mazur grabbed the phone from me as I picked it up. "We will take care of this, Mrs. Hanna. Please I am sorry for the spilled tea. Please go home now. Good-bye."

I started to protest, but he had me by the elbow now and was ushering me out the door. I walked stiffly out into the parking lot. I sat in my car for five minutes. Not one person entered the Spotless Cleaners to offer a hand, nobody from the Nicknack Nook or the pizza place. Nobody rushed to the pay phone. If somebody called 911 on their cell phone, I did not see.

I raced home, and when I got there Thomas was sitting on my porch swing, wearing jeans and a T-shirt that said Save the Humans. I jumped out of the car, babbling about the rock thrown through the window. He stood up and ran down the steps. We hugged like that, with me ranting in the front yard.

"We should call the police," I said, into his shoulder, which smelled of cedar and bourbon.

"I'll go down there," said Thomas. He kissed me on the forehead and hurried to his truck. He rolled down his window and shook a small brown paper bag.

"These are for Pete when he gets home from school."

I took the bag, and reached my hand in like there might be something alive. Inside were a dozen tiny wooden casks.

"They're full of root beer," he said. "I thought he might get a kick out of them. See you later," and he raced off.

The phone was ringing and I hurried inside to get it.

It was Joya. "Did you hear what happened at the cleaners?" she said.

"That poor man. Should I go over there?"

"I think it's under control," I said.

"I'm on my way over there. I'm in the car. By the way, I'm reading a book about raising sons without fathers. It says it's important for little boys to watch a grown-up man shave. Maybe your neighbor could do that for him."

"Thanks Joya. I'll talk to you soon," and I hung up.

I called Mazur at the cleaners, but the phone was off the hook.

Fifteen minutes later, I got a call from Thomas. "The cleaners is boarded up," he said. "Nobody's around. I'm going up to the Hill."

I called Mazur's house, but all I got was a busy signal.

The next morning, the sky was screaming with birds. I sat on the porch sipping coffee as Pete slept. I was wearing just a T-shirt and some lacy underwear I'd sent away for.

The screen door opened and Pete came out dragging his pillow with the dinosaur pillowcase. Joya said there are three kinds of boys—dinosaur boys, snake boys, and train boys—but Pete seemed to be all three. Joya also said it had a direct effect on what kind of husbands they would make, but I had never heard the rest of her theory.

Pete sat next to me on the porch swing, clutching the pillow. "Omar washed his hair in school."

"What do you mean he washed his hair?"

"In the boys' bathroom. I saw him do it, in the sink."

"What did Miss Woodruff say?" I asked.

Pete jumped up and bellowed, *"We do not wash our hair in school. We wash our hair at home."*

"Calm down. Come in and have some breakfast," I said. "Why do you think he did it?"

As we walked back in the house, Pete mumbled, "He said he thought Miss Woodruff would be proud of him."

Mazur called as I was pouring out Frosted Flakes into a bowl.

"How are you?" I said, cradling the phone on my shoulder, and turning away from Pete.

"I can get a new window by tomorrow. I'm sorry you had to see that. We'll have tea again."

"Yes, but do you know who did it?"

"I have to go now," said Mazur, and he hung up.

"Who was that?" said Pete as I handed him his bowl of cereal.

"That was one of my students," I said.

I wandered into the living room and looked out the window into the front yard. The mailman was walking toward our mailbox and it looked like he was wearing surgical gloves.

"Welcome to America, Columbus and his boys," I said.

Pete came running in, with his bowl of cereal, sloshing it on the floor.

"That's not Columbus," he said. "Why is he wearing those special gloves?"

"To keep the mail clean," I murmured.

Pete sat on the couch. "I'm glad I don't have to go to school today," he said, and switched on the radio. "Car Talk" was on, with the two laughing Boston brothers giving advice on how to fix a horn that made the windshield wipers swish violently, every time you honked.

"Those boys would be good to marry us," said Pete.

All weekend I felt like a hummingbird, too nervous to sit still. I drove to the mall with Pete and saw some men installing a new front window at Mazur's shop.

"Did bad guys crash into their window because Omar's uncle crashed the control towers?"

"He did not!" I screamed.

"I'm glad I'm not a twin," said Pete.

Long weekends are not a good idea for single mothers. Thomas was working extra up at the Hill so they wouldn't fire him for all the time spent on his forays to Tennessee, but Monday night we had a date. I even put sour cream on my face Monday afternoon, because Joya swore it made your face feel like silk.

Pete said I smelled like bad milk. In fact, it did make my face feel smoother, but I had to take two showers to take the odor away, which probably dried out my skin more. At 9:30 P.M. when Pete was finally asleep, I appeared on the porch in a little summer shift with turquoise flowers on it and had even painted my toenails berry red.

Thomas drove up in his truck just before ten. He stepped out with a bouquet of autumn leaves and a bottle of wine.

"Sorry I'm late. Maureen called," he said. He took a corkscrew from his back pocket, then squatted down and popped open the cork.

"Would you like a glass?" I said, as Thomas took a swig of wine.

I sat swinging on the swing, clutching the leaves. I wondered if when I got older, I would realize at the time of passion, it would be the last time ever in my life. Would I become an old woman and remember that last time I made love? As Ed lay in his hospital bed in the extra room, it haunted me that I could not remember the precise last time we were together. The hospice worker said there would be a time I would have a hard time remembering his face.

Thomas offered the bottle. I put the leaves next to me and took a swig. Thomas took the bottle from my lips and kissed me.

"Can Pete watch you shave sometime?"

"You can watch me shave sometime," he said, kissing me again. "You're like the forbidden dessert at the back of the refrigerator."

The phone rang.

"Excuse me," I said, getting up. I went inside, but

when I picked up the phone in the kitchen, there was nobody there.

"Hello!" I said. "Hello," I said over and over, but the phone was dead.

Now Pete was calling me from his bed. I tiptoed in and stood by his bed in the dark. He was still lying down, and I bent down and stroked his hair.

"You smell like you're drinking a grown-up drink," he said.

"You should be asleep."

"Will you rub my back?"

"For a minute." I sat down on the bed and rubbed his back. It is strange to leave your lover to go rub your son's back. There is no word for this ritual in English; perhaps there is in another language.

"What's more important than money?" whispered Pete.

"Love," I said.

"No," insisted Pete.

"Yes, it's time to sleep. Love, friends. Lots of things are more important."

"No," said Pete, "only one thing."

"What's that?"

"Water. Water is the most important thing."

I counted to one hundred silently, and then he was asleep.

I wandered through the kitchen and ran my hand along the tins of Martha Stewart herbs and spices I'd ordered from the catalog as Ed lay dying. Joya swears that cancer makes people shop.

When I got back to the porch, Thomas was sitting on the swing drinking wine.

I sat down next to him. "When did you get your job at the Hill?" I said.

"Thirteen years ago. My mother had been in a car crash. She drove even though she couldn't hear. She was killed. I wanted a quiet job. Stay here," he said.

He got up and walked down the porch steps across my yard into his yard, then up his porch steps into his house. I thought he was saying good night, that this revelation about his mother had broken the mood.

But a moment later he was outside dragging a blanket like a small child. He beckoned to me to join him and we went in back of my house and lay down. The blanket was soft and smelled of cedar. As Thomas unzipped my dress he whispered, "Do you think they kissed differently in the eighteenth century?"

We're doing *F* next, said Pete in the morning, as I tickled him awake. "I know *F*. *F* is the Bradley word that rhymes with duck. Foot is another one. And father."

He brought a note home that week in his backpack suggesting children not go out on Halloween because it was a dangerous time, but that there would be a Halloween party at school.

"Oh shot," said Pete, when I read him the note. The year before, when Ed was ranting from the steroids in his hospital bed in the spare room, and I was trying to get Pete to sleep, the kitchen sink clogged and overflowed. I had said *shit*, which I try not to say, and Pete had thought I said *shot*, which I told him was a very, very bad word.

"Oh shot," he said again. "I'm going out on Halloween. I'm going to be a night train engineer."

"What's a night engineer?"

"I'm just going to drive my train at night, so I can stay at home with you during the day. Or, if I need more money, I can sell cars."

"Is this when you grow up or for Halloween?"

"Both," he said.

Halloween fell on a Wednesday, and most of the neighborhood decided it was safe to send the kids out. Mazur called to ask if I could take Omar and baby Henry as well.

When Mazur drove up that evening in his Spotless Cleaners van, Pete ran out to the car in his little blue jeans and blue jean jacket and train engineer's hat. Omar emerged in a cotton Superman costume that had been pressed with creases in the leggings. Mazur stepped out and waved, then reached in the car and handed baby Henry to the boys. Omar and Pete carried the baby practically upside down to the porch.

The boys struggled up the steps, both propping up Henry, and finally dumped him in my lap. "My father has to do 'busyness,' " said Omar.

I took baby Henry inside and put him on my bed. The boys watched as I squished him into a little pumpkin costume with a green stem hood, which Pete had worn when he was a baby.

I had bowls of Tootsie Roll Pops and tiny Milky Ways in the front hall ready for the kids. My plan was to stay home for an hour and receive guests, and then take the boys out. The doorbell rang and Pete and Omar ran to answer it. I followed carrying Henry, the pumpkin boy.

It was Joya, dressed as a belly dancer with a bare midriff and harem pants.

"Where are your kids?" I said through the screen.

"They're in the car. I'm going to a "Single by Chance or by Choice" party. Do you want to come? You really don't waste time," she said, eyeing Henry. "They're having the party at the Y," she continued, pressing her nose to the screen.

"Thanks no, I don't party where I work," I insisted.

I clutched Henry with one arm, opened the door with the other, and handed out the bowl of Tootsie Roll Pops to Joya. She grabbed a bunch for her kids.

"Careful out there," she said. "Omar, you're the neatest Superman I've ever seen. Did your daddy press that?"

"I think my mommy did," said Omar.

After Joya left I took baby Henry into the kitchen and dragged out the high chair I still had in the pantry. I stuck him in it, and opened a can of green beans.

Pete loved to eat those when he was a baby. I lined up a few on the high chair tray and Henry promptly threw them on the floor.

The doorbell rang about eight times over the next hour, and I let Pete and Omar run to greet the neighborhood kids. I stayed in the kitchen with Henry, trying to entertain him. Fortunately he was satisfied in the high chair throwing beans for longer than one might have thought, and I still had Pampers in the hall closet.

I peeked in Pete's room, but the boys were not there. The bathroom door was shut. I knocked, then opened it. There were candy wrappers all over the floor and the shower curtain was pulled closed. I tiptoed in and listened. First I could hear the rustle of candy wrappers being opened in the bathtub. Then I heard Pete yell, "G *is for God, garbage, and goat!*"

"H *is for Halloween, hell, and, and, and, and help!*" Omar shouted back.

They were laughing and laughing, giddy with chocolate.

"Are you boys okay?" I said. "We'll go trick-or-treating in a little while."

The doorbell rang. I hurried to the front door. The porch light shone down on an enormous bear at the door, which looked like it was made of real fur, and it was holding a pumpkin pie in a see-through box.

My first thought was that it was a robber, and then I imagined Ed dressed up to surprise Pete.

"Trick or treat," whispered the bear. It was Thomas.

"Boys!" I called. "Come here. There's a bear at the door."

The boys came running, but froze when they saw the bear through the screen.

Pete pushed open the door. "You're not real. Look at your shoes. You're Thomas!"

It was true. The bear was wearing moccasins.

Thomas handed me the pumpkin pie and took off his bear head and handed it to Pete. The boys rushed back to the bathtub with the head.

Thomas lumbered to the kitchen with the pumpkin pie, and I followed the boys into the bathroom. The curtain was shut again.

"Don't bother us," called Pete. "Do you know what gentlemen do?" I heard him ask Omar.

"What's a gentleman?" said Omar.

"They're always supposed to walk on the outside of a lady in case someone throws garbage on your head, that's what my neighbor Thomas said."

"I never heard that," said Omar.

Baby Henry started crying, and I ran into the kitchen to see Thomas in his bear ensemble lift Henry in his pumpkin suit out of the high chair.

Omar came running into the kitchen, and he was bleeding from his mouth.

Pete followed after him shouting, "I did it! I pulled it out! He asked me to!"

"What the hell?" said Thomas, handing me baby Henry.

Pete opened his hand to reveal a tiny bloody tooth

and handed it to me. Omar opened his mouth to show the space in front where it had been.

"Here, Omar." Thomas took a glass from the cupboard and filled it with water. Then he took the salt shaker from the table and shook in some salt.

"Wash your mouth out with this."

Omar did so obediently.

"Now spit!" said Thomas, and Omar spit into the sink.

"I'll save it for the tooth fairy," I said, rocking back and forth to get baby Henry to stop crying. I rooted around in the top drawer and found an envelope. "I'm a widow," I whispered to Thomas. "My son the dentist, any jobs he can do come in handy . . ."

"I'll give this to your dad when he comes," I said to Omar, sliding the tiny kernel of a tooth into the envelope. "Let's go trick-or-treating before it's too late."

The boys ran out to get their shoes, and baby Henry started making happy gurgling sounds.

The boys were at the front door, in full regalia, with their shoes on, I was holding Henry in his pumpkin suit, and Thomas was putting on his bear head, when Mazur pulled up in his van.

"Omar must come home now," he said running up the front path to the porch. "Somebody smashed the window again."

I ran to get the envelope with Omar's tooth before his father grabbed Henry with one hand and took Omar by the other.

That night the bear went trick-or-treating with my

son, the night train engineer. I sat on the couch in the living room eating pumpkin pie from the pie box, watching CNN interview a doctor about anthrax. I got up five times to greet costumed children. The sixth time I went to the door it was Maureen. She was dressed as a waitress, with a little paper hat. I did not know if it was a costume or for a real job.

"Hi, Maureen," I said. "Would you like to come in?"

"What's it like having a baby?"

"Are you sure you don't want to come in?"

A gang of tiny ghosts and witches were clambering up the porch stairs.

"Trick or treat! Trick or treat!" they yelled.

"I want my baby to hear, right? I'm not crazy, right?"

The kids were at the door now scratching on the screen around Maureen.

"Please come in," I said, meaning to Maureen, but the kids opened the door and pushed in to grab candy.

Maureen stood outside in her waitress uniform. Her little paper hat had gone askew.

"How old are you?" I said quietly.

"Fifteen," she said flatly.

"Wait there," I said. I turned my back to make sure the kids hadn't thrown all the candy into their bags. I shooed the children out, and Maureen walked in hesitantly and slid down on the couch. She looked like an old woman now.

"How's your job? It's your job, right?" I asked.

"Denny's. I don't think I'm going to last," she drifted off, nibbling on a Tootsie Roll.

"I think you're brave," I said.

"Brave? To get knocked up and work at Denny's? I'll say I'm brave."

"Brave to leave home," I said. "Look at me. I grew up here."

"Maybe they'll give me a medal," said Maureen.

"I'm not telling you not to. I'm just asking you a question. Are you sure you want the baby?"

Maureen nodded.

"Do you want to sleep here?" I said. "On a bed?"

"No thank you. I like my car."

NOVEMBER

NOVEMBRE

Morning broke on November 1st with a full sun shining in a cool blue sky. It was a glorious day, as if God had finally gotten a good night's sleep. I let Pete eat peanut butter cookies he'd gotten in his Halloween bag for breakfast, before he raced off to the bus. That day I gave my students the assignment of "Memory of Your First Bedroom," but I could not get the image of Maureen out of my head. She was only ten years older than Pete. Friday, I put in some overtime hours at the library and Pete brought in his father's slippers to kindergarten for show-and-tell. When I got back from work, there was a ladder leaned up against my house. When I shut the porch door, I realized Thomas had taken down all the screens and put up the storm windows in their place.

There was a note on the porch swing: "Meet me up at the Hill." I went to the kitchen and grabbed the rest of the pumpkin pie, and went back out to the porch swing with a fork. After I finished off the whole pie, I lay down and closed my eyes, as I waited for Pete's bus.

The bus pulled up at three-twenty, and Pete bounded off it with his backpack swinging from his arm. "Don't shut your eyes! You look dead!" he called as he threw his backpack at me and ran inside. I sat up and unzipped the pack. There was one library book and a note in his folder. The kindergarteners were allowed to check out one book each week, and for the third time he had selected *The Wildlife of Wisconsin*.

The note read:

Dear Parents,
     There will be a Thanksgiving feast in school on the Wednesday before Thanksgiving. Please bring in the item or items checked below (enough for twenty-eight children!).

My assignment was mashed sweet potatoes with marshmallows.

"We're going to the supermarket," I called to Pete. I decided I'd buy the sweet potatoes and marshmallows early. When I was a child we used to have a ritual of playing bingo after dinner with my aunts and uncles, which I enjoyed. Thanksgiving with Ed was always at my in-laws' house, a large meal at Ed's father's or one of his sister's where they always served duck. When Pete was three, he took the meat from his plate and slid it into his sock. This year I had no plans except for the kindergarten feast, to which parents were not invited.

I went inside to try and lure Pete out of his room. He was lying on the floor lining up cars in a traffic jam.

"C'mon," I coaxed. "I'll buy you a Lunchable."

This was one of the junk foods that Pete craved, and it was often a good bribe.

"A dessert Lunchable," he said, not looking up from his cars.

In *Widows of the World*, I had read that a Hindu woman is stigmatized as a woman who has failed to safeguard her husband's life should he die. I wanted to tell Pete that it was not my fault that his father died, but instead I agreed to the dessert Lunchable.

On the drive to the supermarket, Pete said, "When I grow up, I'm going to wear a special uniform and punch bees."

"Okay," I said. "If I ever get married again, I don't ever, ever want to get divorced."

"I want you to be divorced," said Pete, kicking my seat.

"Why?"

" 'Cause then I could spend some time alone with my dad. That's what Joya's kids do."

The supermarket was at the far end of the shopping center away from Spotless Cleaners and the pizza place. I parked and as soon as we got out, Pete began pulling on my arm, toward the cleaners.

"I want to see if Omar's there," Pete insisted.

"We need stuff for Thanksgiving," I pleaded.

"Mom," said Pete. "Miss Woodruff said you don't have to do that homework for a lot of weeks."

I complied and walked nervously down the sidewalk, past the Drug-Mart, past the Doughnut-Dock, past the Pet Palace where we'd gotten Mimo. I could see, from in front of Cadillac Nails, that a new window had been installed at the cleaners.

"We really should get the sweet potatoes," I said, but I headed toward the cleaners like I was sleepwalking.

Mazur was outside, quietly paying some men for putting up the new glass.

He greeted us formally and even coaxed Pete to shake his hand. I moved close to Mazur, as if he were a shield, and then a red minivan slowed down and the window rolled down. The woman in the passenger seat was wearing a visor on her head from a theme park near Chicago.

"Goddamn Arabs and Jews," she muttered as the car passed.

I covered Pete's ears with my hands, even though the car had driven off.

Pete pulled my hands away from his head.

"Would you like to come in for tea?" said Mazur. "Omar is with his aunt. He is not here, but I have some cookies." He held out his hand to Pete, and we trailed into the Spotless Cleaners like it was our home.

The cleaning smell seemed stronger than usual, and Pete immediately held his nose.

Pete marched after Mazur to the room behind the counter, and within seconds he was bouncing up and down on the little red couch. I walked tentatively behind, like I was going into a brothel. Mazur attempted to pour me tea again without violence. He did fill the cup, but the little bell at the front of the shop rang. Soon I could hear a woman talking to his cousin.

"I know your family is under a lot of stress," flirted the woman, and there was no doubt that the voice belonged to Joya.

I wanted to hide back there, but Pete stopped bouncing and ran to the front of the store.

"Joya," he shouted. "There's a special room back here!"

I walked to the doorway and gave a little wave. Mazur stood right behind me.

"Would you enjoy some tea?"

"Sorry, I didn't mean to interrupt," she said, raising her eyebrows. "I thought you didn't enjoy tea," she said pointedly to me.

The bell rang again, and Thomas walked in with a pile of muslin clothes in his arms.

"We're having a party," said Joya.

"I thought you were coming up to the Hill," he said, not looking at me as he dumped his clothes on the counter, and it occurred to me that there were stains from our passion somewhere in that pile.

"Thank you," I said to Mazur. "Thank you for the tea," although again I had not taken a sip.

Pete was at the front window, using the wedding dress hanging in plastic as a punching bag. "Where's Omar? Where's Omar? Can Omar come over?" he said.

Mazur and I stood behind the counter. Thomas reached out his hand to take a receipt for the clothes.

I was not sure where to stand, so I said, "Pete, stop punching that dress. C'mon. It's time to go home."

I walked to the front of the counter and Thomas ran his arm along my leg as I passed him. I pulled Pete from his punching-bag dress.

"Thank you," I waved to Joya and Mazur, and I pulled Pete out of the store. Thomas followed me and put his arm around me, so Mazur and Joya could see us through the big window.

"I have to go work for a new distillery for the next few weeks. It's good money," said Thomas.

"I'm worried about Maureen," I said.

Thomas nodded. "Twice when I was younger than Pete, I was locked out of the house at night, because my parents couldn't hear me calling them." Thomas lifted Pete and put him on his shoulders. "So," he said. "Do you have a thing for Mazur?"

"No," I said as we walked to our cars. "He's a friend."

"He's got a crunch on you," said Pete.

Thomas walked us to our car. He put his hand on my neck and said, "I'll be back by Thanksgiving.

There's always a big dinner up at the Hill, and great fireworks. Would you like to go?"

"Yes! We won't lock you out," said Pete, raising his fists above his head.

I drove home wearily. We did not get to the super-market that day.

Time folded in on itself the weeks before Thanks-giving. The only thing that kept me from losing track was Pete's alphabet homework. Each night I couldn't sleep. After a week of dancing endlessly to country-and-western music in my nightgown at 3 A.M. in the kitchen, I sneaked over to Thomas's house and sat on his porch. I realized that I needed to get out of town. That night I made a decision. Pete and I would take a short vacation. I had never traveled alone with him before.

Monday, November 12, would have been Ed's forty-sixth birthday. I decided to take Pete to Niagara Falls in Ed's honor. Ed and I used to joke that we would go there on our fiftieth wedding anniversary. Monday morning I went to teach at the YMCA and told my students that I had to attend to family matters and needed a few days off. My supervisor at the library said, "You've been looking a little pale." As a widow I could get away with a certain amount of these excuses. Joya said, "You have a year to act as strange as you want, then all bets are off." She would feed the cat.

I had a map, but reading maps was Ed's department. I stopped at the gas station and spoke to Chris Cotter. I went to school with Chris, and although he never graduated, he had a gift for reading maps, which was revealed in the fifth grade when our bus driver got lost on a class trip to a button factory. I spent almost a half hour at the gas station, slowly writing down the directions to the falls, as he stood next to me in his oil-stained clothes and gave me directions a child could follow.

I then stopped at the supermarket to buy several boxes of Lunchables as bait for Pete and bought the five pounds of sweet potatoes and four bags of marshmallows for the Thanksgiving feast.

I packed minimally—sweatshirts for both of us, a box of rescue vehicles for Pete, and his pillow with the dinosaur pillowcase.

"I'll go to jail for skipping school," said Pete at dinner when I told him my plan.

"Don't worry. We'll be back in a couple of days. I'll carry you to the car while you're still asleep tomorrow morning. Daddy used to do that when you were a baby."

"Daddy was stronger," he said.

"You can sleep in your clothes," I offered.

Tuesday morning I rose at 4 A.M and put on one of my long denim skirts and a Reds T-shirt. I made enough coffee to fill two thermoses and salami sandwiches to eat on the way.

I did manage to carry the slumbering child to the

car, although I practically fell down the porch stairs.

Pete kicked my seat for fifteen minutes, but then slept through the darkness. As I drove I had pictures in my head of Maureen driving with a newborn baby by her side in her powder-blue Mustang. The sun came up, and it was Wednesday morning in America and we passed car after car of women driving with their children in the backseat. I felt as if I was in some kind of special motorcade.

I stopped for gas and Pete lifted his little head like a newborn, but then lay back down again.

We arrived at 10 A.M., at Niagara Falls, the American side. Pete stayed rooted to the backseat, when I opened the door like a wing. Arctic air blasted in on us. I lifted my crumpled body and stepped out into the icy parking lot. Raw wind sailed up my legs.

The falls were magnificent, white and loud the way God had meant them to be, thundering water, crashing down into icicles. Farther down the railing was one lone scarecrow of a man in a black snowmobile suit, who looked like he might jump. I shut my eyes and whispered, "Happy birthday, Ed."

Pete was up now, shivering by my side. "*I* is for ice, igloo, and more ice," he mumbled.

Most intelligent people were inside with blankets piled on top of them, but there were two couples pressed to the railing, looking out.

"Happy birthday, Ed," I said again.

"We need to get him a cake," said Pete seriously.

We stayed at the falls for about a half hour, then

headed back to the car to search for cake.

"I wish Daddy could drive," said Pete.

We immediately found a diner called the Parrot Paradise, and I skidded into the parking lot. We hurried up the steps, clapping our hands to keep warm. Inside we slid into a big booth. The jukebox was playing "A Hard Day's Night." A large display case filled with ten-inch-high cakes turned slowly around.

The waitress, who looked to be Maureen's age, came by and took our order.

"Three pieces of that chocolate cake please, milk for my son, and I'll have coffee. Thank you."

"It's my dad's birthday," said Pete sleepily to the waitress.

"Will he be joining you?" said the waitress, ripping our bill from her pad.

She did not wait for us to answer. I believe she'd seen everything. She brought our order, with a lit candle in one of the pieces of cake, which she put across from Pete, as if Ed might really show up. Pete slowly pulled it toward him, so he had two pieces in front of him. We sang "Happy Birthday" and nobody even turned to look. Then Pete insisted on singing "Are you one? Are you two? Are you three?" all the way up to forty-six, as I sipped my coffee, and stared out at the icy day. Pete ended up eating Ed's piece.

We found a bowling alley, which had a video arcade that looked like it might be the headquarters for a kidnapping ring, and we bowled. Even with his cockeyed five-year-old throws, Pete beat me 97–28. For a reward, and because I wanted to use the phone, I let Pete play those awful arcade machines. I fed him quarters, and he parked himself at something called "Crazy Taxi." I kept one eye on him, walking backward until I found a pay phone. I called Joya to see how everything was.

I confided about Maureen being pregnant and all, and that her parents were deaf and the baby might be deaf as well. She told me that people in Ash Creek had begun boycotting Mazur's cleaners.

"How can they? Where else is there to go?" I said, as Pete came over and tried to grab quarters from my pockets.

"There's a new place opening on the strip, run by Larry Williams. Remember in tenth grade he decorated his locker with condoms?"

"I'll be back by tomorrow," I said.

In the afternoon we found a motel with a round bed, where Pete ate several Lunchables. We both fell into a deep sleep until 6 A.M., when we were awakened by a couple having sex in the room next door.

Pete said, "I think someone is being killed. We better leave before they kill us."

On the long, long drive back to Ohio, Pete insisted on helping me put gas in the car, which meant me trying to grab the nozzle so we wouldn't spray gas all over the ground. At a gas station somewhere in Pennsylvania, it was warm enough for him to squeegee, one of his hobbies, so I let him wash the windows. I sat in the car, letting the child carefully smudge the windshield. Pete marched up to me with the squeegee raised and knocked on my window. I rolled it down.

"You should have saved a piece of Daddy's hair so I could have it," he said.

"I should have. I'm sorry. Now get in," and I rolled the window back up.

On the night after we returned from Niagara Falls, I only slept two tossing hours. The other endless time I lay on the bed, watching the clock. I began to wish God had not invented night at all, but instead had made great double days with no idea of night at all.

Pete went back to school and I staggered back to work. "*J* is for jump, jelly bean, jail," said Pete before he fell asleep the second night back.

It was true what Joya had said about the boycott. I drove out to the strip and saw a new cleaners, Aphrodite Alpine Cleaners, on the way to work. There was a big American flag in the window.

When I got home from teaching, I went through all our closets and yanked out more clothes than I'd ever taken to the cleaners at once. I even found a boiled wool baby coat of Pete's that had been a gift from one of Ed's relatives and was so itchy no human child had ever worn it. I lifted the large mound of clothes and hurled them into the backseat of the car, then speeded over to Mazur's shop, wanting to save his life.

"How is your wife?" I said when I handed Mazur the huge pile.

"She is coming home," he said.

That night, I was sitting with Pete on his bed, reading *The Wildlife of Wisconsin* to him, when the phone rang.

Pete jumped up to answer it. "ThisisPetewhoisthisplease?" and then he brought the phone into his room. "Why do you want to talk to my mom?" I heard him say.

Then he yelled to me, "Thomas says he bought me a fishing rod, because he didn't give me anything for my birthday."

The evening before the Thanksgiving feast at school, Pete and I spent all evening mashing sweet potatoes. Orange mush was all over the kitchen walls and floor. The cat licked it up like it was catnip. I cooked huge wads of marshmallows so the kitchen smelled of burned sugar. Then we filled every shape Tupperware ever invented with the delicacy. When friends had brought those Tupperware containers after Ed died, I had great trouble believing that he was dead. Now I had the strange sensation of not being able to recall that he ever lived.

Thomas came home at 3 A.M. on Thanksgiving day. I was up, trying to scrub the orange mess from the kitchen. He just walked into the kitchen in his muslin clothes, carrying Pete's fishing rod, and opened the refrigerator.

"Hi, honey," he said, and then we went to bed.

Thanksgiving was one of the most bustling days of the year up at the Hill, according to Thomas. Something about the holiday gave people a more agitated yearning for a homespun way of life. Thomas got up early. I pretended to be asleep as he tiptoed out of the room.

I peeked out the window to see him walk across the backyards to his kitchen door, wearing his pants and carrying his muslin shirt and moccasins. I went in to check on Pete. He was fast asleep, but completely turned around, so his feet were on his dinosaur pillow. Thomas had leaned the prize fishing rod against his bed.

The Thanksgiving meal was to be at 1 P.M. All morning Pete fished for leaves in the backyard.

I spent a few hours reading my students' work, interspersed with getting up and calling out the kitchen door at Pete not to get caught on the hook. I also called Mazur's house and shop several times, but nobody picked up. At noon, I got into the shower to prepare myself for my first Thanksgiving with people I did not know.

I was washing my "bretsis," when Pete dangled the fishing rod into the tub. "Get out of here!" I demanded.

"Just like Columbus and his boys," said Pete, "Can we go fishing today?"

"Get out of the bathroom, and we'll talk then," I said, with my hands trying to cover myself.

Pete finally got out, but left the door open. "I could see your private parts anyway," he said.

"No, we can't go fishing. It's Thanksgiving. We're going up to the Hill for a big meal."

I stepped out of the tub, dried myself, and wrapped the towel around my head. Then I threw on my bathrobe and scurried into my bedroom.

Pete was lying under my bed and peeked his head out. I cinched my bathrobe tighter.

"Get out!" I pleaded. "Could you please put on a clean shirt?"

"What are you, a Muslim?" he said, and ran out of the room with his fishing rod.

I put on some of my new underwear, then my skirt and blouse and some rosewater perfume that I thought would be appropriate for a colonial meal.

"I had a feast yesterday at school," said Pete flopping on the couch. "I'm not going."

"If you don't put on a clean shirt with at least three buttons, I'll give the fishing rod back to Thomas."

Pete stomped into his room and emerged with a blue polo shirt with two buttons. One was missing, but it was close enough.

"Come on," I yelled, and finally I was able to corral him into the car.

It was a beautiful day, with a cool breeze, but clear

skies. You would have thought the circus had come to town. The parking lot was jammed up at the Hill. People were in their good clothes, shirts and ties and even some high heels, sinking into the November earth, marching toward the manor house. It would be a buffet, but still it was a big event.

We had to buy tickets at the gift shop, and then we could go directly into the formal dining room.

All kinds of olden-day food was laid out on the long, oak table—game birds and bowls of dangerous-looking stuffings. There were bottles and bottles of port and liqueurs and ciders and trays and trays of meringues and little cakes. A line was already forming when we got there.

I deemed immediately that we would eat outside.

"Where's Thomas. Where's Thomas?" Pete kept saying, as I pulled him from butting ahead in line.

We filled our paper plates and I steered Pete outside to sit on a three-hundred-year-old wall. I hadn't seen Thomas yet. He was scheduled to give a small lecture at the cooper's shop and had said he would join us when he was done.

I was chewing on some kind of partridge and Pete was pushing his food around on his plate, talking about Lunchables.

"Do you think people in the olden days sat on this wall?" I said.

Pete dropped his fork on the ground and muttered, "Something smells."

"Don't be rude," I said, bending down to pick up

his fork. "People spent a lot of time preparing this food."

"I smell smoke," said Pete.

I stood up, and squinted my eyes. The boy was right. It appeared that the barn was on fire. I strained my eyes and could now see red furious flames. I pulled Pete by the hand as our plates spilled to the ground.

"Don't litter!" he ordered. I pulled Pete toward the cooper's shed.

Explosions were going off like small bombs in the air. It took me several minutes before I realized we were not being attacked. It took slightly longer to comprehend that the sounds were from the stash of fireworks exploding.

I had never seen such a large fire before. It was a red and wild fire and Pete was chanting, "Ladybug, ladybug, fly away home, your house is on fire and your children have flown."

Thomas rushed by with two buckets slung over his shoulder like a real colonial man. Carloads of frightened people were streaming out of the parking lot.

"Get out of here!" yelled Thomas over his shoulder.

"Maybe we should lie down and roll home," said Pete.

"We're driving," I said.

"You said there'd be fireworks," said Pete running next to me.

The smoke was putrid now. We made it to the parking lot and I frantically rummaged in my purse for the keys. Cows were mooing heartsick in the fields. I found my keys and shoved Pete into the car.

"You shouldn't push. Pushing is rude," he muttered, as we raced down the hill. I looked at the fiery barn in the rearview mirror and prayed that Thomas would not die.

Pete sat in the back, and kicked my seat. "Is Thomas going to burn? Is Thomas going to burn up?" he said softly.

Fire alarms began to clang through the air. On the way toward our house, we passed three fire trucks with their sirens on full blast.

"I want to visit Omar and his father," said Pete in a small voice, and I did not disagree. We slowed down in front of our house and then Thomas's house like we were with a Realtor looking at new homes.

I pressed my foot to the gas and headed out of town to the mall. As I drove, Pete sang in a small voice, "Oh do you know the muffin man, the muffin man, the muffin man, oh do you know the muffin man who lives on Drury Lane?"

An American mall on Thanksgiving is desolate by design, so I could drive right up to Mazur's shop. It looked closed. I parked but kept the motor running. I could see Mazur inside, counting receipts. Omar was with him, sitting on the counter.

I turned off the motor, and as we got out I hissed to Pete, "Now please act normal."

Pete rapped on the window and Mazur immediately let us in.

"What happened? Are you alright? I heard the sirens." Mazur put his hand lightly on my shoulder.

Pete bolted in ahead of me and climbed up on the counter next to Omar.

"It's up at the Hill. It's burning down."

Mazur put his head in his hands. "Is everybody okay?"

Mazur and I went to the back room and sat down next to each other on the red couch. He put his arms around me and we hugged like that, nothing more, as the boys played store in the front.

That night, I agreed to let Pete have his first sleepover at Omar's house. Mazur assured me they'd be fine. I went home to spend the first time in five years without my son. I took a long bath and lit a ginger candle, and listened to the local radio station. All of the colonial buildings were burning to the ground. Nothing was able to be saved. The reports said over and over that nobody was hurt, not even the livestock, but still I was frightened about Thomas.

After my bath, I ate some leftover sweet potato and marshmallows. When I was stuffed, I went out and paced on the porch like I was on a widow's walk and my sailor was lost at sea.

Just before 9 P.M., Thomas staggered up the front walkway with a sooty face and ashes in his hair like a scarecrow.

He slumped down on the porch swing next to me and patted my hand. "Probably linseed oil rags; they'd been doing some renovations. That and the fireworks. I don't know . . . Could have been a tourist smoking."

And then he cried.

The next morning at 6 A.M. it was raining softly. I left Thomas in a deep sleep in my bed and drove cautiously up to the Hill.

When I reached the parking lot, I turned off the motor but stayed in the car. Raindrops filled the windshield as I stared out at the smoky skeleton of the manor house. The barn and the charred remnants of the cooper's shed and blacksmith shop were not recognizable. The remains looked like the bones of washed-up whales in the fields. I rolled down my window. The air smelled of burned-up firecrackers and the sweet stash of bayberry and beeswax candles.

When I got back home, Thomas and Pete were in the kitchen examining the rock candy in the jar of water. Their heads were bent toward each other, touching, like they were conjoined twins.

"Pete," I said. "How was your first sleepover? You're back so early. Was everything okay?"

Neither Thomas nor Pete looked up, but Pete said, "Baby Henry cried a lot, and Omar's father said he had to take me home, because he had to make plants or plans, I don't know. His mommy's back. She's not dead."

Thomas looked up at me with sad eyes. He looked older. He had showered, but his face still looked gray. He must have gone to his house to get fresh clothes.

"I'll have to find another job," he said.

I nodded.

The front door banged open and shut and Joya entered our kitchen. She was wearing a coat but it was open and you could see she was wearing an orange tank top with her jeans.

She stood leaning against the sink, nuzzling up to Thomas and Pete. "They're saying it was set by Arabs," she said.

"That's ridiculous," said Thomas. "Linseed rags, probably—a loose match."

"Well, people are saying it's Arabs."

The phone rang. It was Mazur. "We're moving," he said. "May I come to say good-bye with you?"

I could feel tears in the back of my eyes. "Where? Why? Are you sure?"

"Yes," he said. "We have relatives in Edgewater, New Jersey. They own a gas station. Have you visited there in Edgewater, New Jersey?"

"No, I never have," I murmured.

"Will you visit? We did not set the fire."

"I know that," I said.

When I hung up, Joya just raised her eyebrows. Thomas didn't say anything, so I started making a batch of pancakes. Pete pulled Thomas away from the rock candy, out the kitchen door.

As I stirred the batter, I watched Thomas show Pete

how to cast the fishing rod out into the rainy November sky.

"Mazur is leaving town," I said quietly to Joya. She sat down at the kitchen table, took off one shoe, and began to massage her foot.

"I should get back to my kids," she said. "I left them asleep."

After Joya left, I called Pete and Thomas in for pancakes.

"We ate some sweet potatoes and marshmallows already," Thomas called back.

I stood at the sink, eating pancakes with my hands.

An hour later Mazur came by and honked like an American. I stepped out onto the porch and I could see a woman was with him in the front seat. The fishermen were still at their task. Omar jumped out of the van and ran to the backyard. Mazur stepped out and walked methodically around to the passenger side to open the door for his wife. She put her crutches out first, then slowly got out of the car, wearing an exquisite turquoise sari. Mazur opened the back door to unstrap baby Henry from his seat. They carefully made their way up the front path.

Mazur's wife was beautiful. She looked about twenty-five, graceful, even with the crutches, with deep-set haunted eyes.

"I would like you to meet my wife," said Mazur, clutching baby Henry in one hand.

"I'm so sorry for your loss," I murmured.

She looked at the ground. "Thank you for caring for my children."

"You have food in your hair," Mazur said quietly to me. He reached up his hand but did not touch my head.

"Pancakes. Excuse me," I said, patting at my head, not knowing exactly where the batter was. "Would you like some?"

"No, we will be going to Edgewater, New Jersey, now. We will be back for our things. My wife wants Omar to start school there right away."

Mazur called for his son, and Omar ran to the front immediately.

It started to pour now, and Thomas and Pete came running up the steps. Thomas put the fishing rod safely in the corner against the house, then we all huddled on the porch.

I tried to make introductions, but I didn't know Mazur's wife's name, so instead I said, "This is Omar's mother," and Thomas said, "I'm sorry," and Pete was saying, "I don't want them to move, I don't want them to move."

Mazur and Thomas shook hands like they had just made a bet.

"Good luck with you," said Mazur. "I hope you are finding a new job."

"I hope that for you, too," said Thomas, and both men looked away from each other.

Pete and Omar held hands like they were going on

a class trip together and suddenly began to sing as we all stared out at the rain. They sang their own rendition of "America."

"My country 'tis of thee, sweet land of liverty (Pete always said liverty), of thee I sing." And then they both sang softly, "Land where our fathers died, land where the pilgrims cried, from every mountainside, let freedom rink."

Mazur hugged me with baby Henry between us, and Thomas put his hands lightly on my back. For a moment we stood like a strange sandwich. Then Mazur took Omar by his free hand. Thomas helped Mazur's wife down the slippery steps and they all made their way through the rain to Mazur's van.

As Mazur started the van, Thomas ran back onto the porch and Pete darted out into the wet yard and under the porch. I waved as Mazur and his family drove off, but only Omar waved back.

Thomas sat down on the porch swing and shut his eyes.

I let Pete have his privacy for about ten minutes, while I stared out at the quiet street. The mailman walked up to our mailbox wearing his pith helmet and plastic gloves.

Then I tiptoed down the steps and crept under the porch. "What are you doing?" I said.

Pete was holding a gardening shovel. "I want to dig up Daddy," he said.

"C'mon out and let's talk about it," I said, although I did not have a clue what to say.

Pete marched out from under the porch with his shovel, climbed up on the porch, and sat next to Thomas on the swing.

"I think we should go on a trip," said Thomas, opening his eyes. "It's Thanksgiving vacation."

"Where?" I sighed.

"Kitty Hawk," said Thomas. "That's where you said you wanted to go on your fiftieth birthday. Why wait?"

"I want a kitten," said Pete.

"No, Kitty Hawk, it's where two brothers, who invented the first airplane, flew through the sky. They lived in Ohio, too," I said.

"In the olden days?" said Pete waving his shovel around.

"In the olden days," said Thomas.

The next day, Friday morning, Thomas telephoned from his house. "Maureen would like to come with us. Is that alright? We'd have to use your car. We couldn't all fit in the truck."

I looked out the kitchen window at the November trees. "Yes," I said. "Why not?"

We agreed we would leave by ten o'clock. Pete packed his backpack full of Legos and plastic dinosaurs and one small stuffed boy soccer player he'd been sleeping with. "It's a doll," he said, "but if anybody asks, don't tell them it's a doll."

When I called Joya to ask if she'd feed the cat, I did not mention that Maureen was coming with us. My suitcase was dusty, but I dragged it down from the closet and packed jeans and T-shirts for Pete and myself, and stuffed my new bras underneath.

Pete was spraying his bicycle with the hose, because Thomas said he'd put the bike rack on my car. While I was dumping dozens of unused chemo pills down the toilet, I heard a car drive up. I figured it was Joya, so I continued rummaging through the medicine cabinet, looking for tiny tubes of toothpaste and bottles of shampoo.

"Mom!" Pete called to me from the front yard.

I did not answer him, because I really wanted him to learn to come get me when he needed me, not bellow at me like I was a servant girl.

"Mom!" he called again.

When I got out to the porch I said, "I'm tired of you screaming at me," in a controlled voice. "What is it?"

Pete was walking with a letter up the front path.

"A lady left something in the mailbox," he said. "Do you want me to deliver it to you?"

"Yes, thank you," I said.

"Wait, not yet," said Pete. He ran into the house with the letter and came back with my yellow rubber dishwashing gloves, which I kept under the sink and rarely wore. He placed the envelope on the top step of the porch and struggled to put on the gloves.

"There," he said, waving his big yellow hands around. "Delivery, here's the mail. Now I look like the real mailman."

"Thank you, sir," I said.

I took the envelope.

"Who's it from?" he said. "Is it a birthday party? Whose birthday is it?" as I ripped it open.

It was not a letter. It was a page torn from a spiral notebook. There was a note written in big block letters on the lined paper.

K IS FOR KANGAROO, KILL, KIKE

I was dizzy.

"Whose birthday?" said Pete over and over. "Whose birthday?"

"Oh," I shook my head, crumpling the paper. "It's just an advertisement for something."

"For what's it an advertisement?"

"To clean cars," I said, staring out at the empty road.

"You should keep it," he said, grabbing at the paper. "I like to clean cars."

"No!" I insisted, holding tight to the paper. "Go get Thomas now."

Pete ran over to Thomas's house and Thomas came out to his porch. He had a wrench in his hand.

"What is it?" he said. "I'm fixing the kitchen faucet. Maureen will be here soon. Are you ready?"

I was shaking. "We're ready to go," I mumbled. I turned and stomped into the house, tearing the note into little pieces. I went into the bathroom and flushed it down the toilet with the chemo medicine.

Maureen pulled up in her powder-blue Mustang a few minutes later. I peeked out the bathroom window at her. She was dressed for the beach, like we'd already arrived in North Carolina. She was wearing one of her bare-midriff sleeveless T-shirts, cutoff jeans, and flip-flops with a large plastic sunflower between the toes. As she got out of the car, I could see that she was pregnant. Her navel ring looked like it might pop out any minute.

I flushed the toilet again and went out to greet her.

"Will you be warm enough?" I said.

"I'm hot all the time now." She reached for a pack of cigarettes from her bag.

"I'm going to have to ask you not to smoke in the car, and around Pete," I said.

"Any more laws?" she said, stuffing the cigarettes back in her bag.

"That's about it," I said. "Can I help you with your bag?"

Maureen looked at me longer in the eye than she ever had before, and I thought she might cry. "Thank you," she said. "I just have my duffel."

Thomas came out and hoisted Pete's bike on my car and then his own. I ran back in the house and checked the stove and coffeemaker, then came back out and locked up the house.

"Good-bye house," I whispered, touching the door frame. "Good-bye, Ed."

The kids got in the backseat like we were going to Disneyland, and I got in the passenger's seat.

"Don't let my mother drive," demanded Pete, as Thomas sped out of town.

"I won't," said Thomas.

"Do you know how to get there?" I said, and closed my eyes.

"West Virginia. Virginia. North Carolina. We'll be at the beach by dinnertime."

"Where will we sleep?" said Pete, kicking his seat.

"You kick that seat once more and you'll sleep on the roof."

"We'll find a place," I assured him. I turned around. Maureen was already asleep.

The Wright brothers' trip was more tedious. First they took a train, then a steamer to Norfolk, Virginia. Then they took another train and finally a small boat into Kitty Hawk Bay. There were no bridges then to connect the Outer Banks of North Carolina to the mainland. I knew Wilbur and Orville's route precisely, but I did not have a clue on how to drive there myself.

Thomas did not consult me anyway. He drove like a demon and I sat there like a dazed housewife. I wanted to tell him about the note in the mailbox, but Pete was still awake.

He drove and drove and when Pete finally fell asleep, he reached over and took my hand.

"I don't want to go back home," I said.

Thomas kept his eyes straight ahead. "What are we going to do? Be fishermen?"

"Maybe," I said. "I just want to start fresh somewhere."

"We came down here for wind and sand, and we have got them," wrote Orville Wright to his sister on

October 18, 1900. Their mother had died long before they flew their aeroplane.

Thomas skidded into the parking lot of The Aviator Motel in Duck, North Carolina. We'd found the sand. The kids were still asleep and we stepped out into the salty wind. It was warmer than in Ohio. I ran to the beach as Thomas went inside to check out the rooms.

I stood on the sand and faced the Atlantic for the first time. The waves were crashing on the shore the way I thought they would, but the sky seemed wider. Seagulls were screaming, swirling around some washed-up fish on the beach. I breathed out as if I'd been holding my breath for a long time.

Thomas came up behind me and put his hands on my shoulders.

"It's off-season, I got two rooms. Kids in one. We'll take the other."

I nodded. "I've never done this before."

"Gone to a motel with your neighbor and his niece?"

"No," I said. "Gone to the ocean. I've never seen the Atlantic before."

"It's not possible," he said, but he could see I was telling the truth.

Maureen emerged from the car looking like a little girl and hugged herself. I took off my sweatshirt and held it out to her like an olive branch as she approached, and she put it on without making a sound.

"I'm starving," she said, barely looking at the ocean. "Why the hell are we here anyway?" she said, as she stalked back to the car.

I ran to the car and reached in to shake Pete awake.

"It's the ocean," I said. "Come look." I pulled him by the hand and he followed in a daze.

As we stood on the beach, he said, "You know, that's the same water since when the dinosaurs were here. It's all recycled. Same water."

"Who told you that?"

"I'm not lying," he said. "Mrs. Irwin told us in music, and then we had to sing a song about pollution. They could send me to jail for not going to school."

"It's still the weekend," I assured him. "C'mon, we're going to get something to eat."

We carried our things into the motel. The rooms smelled of saltwater and toilet-bowl cleaner. After the kids had each claimed a bed, we got ourselves back into the car.

We passed a few boarded-up restaurants, and shell shops, and then Thomas pulled into The Harbor House, with a big sign that read All U Ca Eat, with the *n* missing in "can," but we got the picture.

"I crave fried clams," said Maureen.

"I crave them, too," said Pete.

We were the only ones in the place, except for two very large waitresses clearing tables in slow motion. We spent an hour there. Pete and Maureen appeared to be engaged in some eating race of overly fried foods. I ate crab cakes for the first time, two rounds, and Thomas had three bowls of fish gumbo, while we played footsie under the table.

It was only that night in bed, in the dark, that I told him about the note in the mailbox.

"Who did it, do you think?" I whispered.

"Maybe the same person who set the fire."

I sat up, and pulled the little curtain back so I could look out at the dark Atlantic. "I thought you said that was an accident."

"I didn't want to tell you," he said.

"What?"

"They had been getting anti-Arab notes up at the Hill."

"But why there?"

"Who knows why. They'd recently hired a guy from somewhere in the Middle East, to be a caretaker. Nice guy. Who knows why."

"Who knows why," I murmured.

Saturday morning Thomas and I woke early and walked on the beach.

"Let's live here," I said.

"And do what? Work in All U Ca Eat?" said Thomas, kicking a piece of driftwood.

When the kids got up, we headed for the Wright Brothers Museum and Kill Devil Hills, where the brothers took their first flight. It was a small museum, run by the parks department, with a parking lot the size of a 7-Eleven.

We paid a park ranger for tickets, and headed in to see the amazing planes with their cloth wings on ribs like old-fashioned corsets. There were two tall tourists from Holland, with backpacks, talking clattering Dutch. Otherwise we had the place to ourselves. Each display case held a treasure. One case had the brothers' beautiful suits and derby hats. Another held their binoculars. On the wall was the article from *Gleanings in Bee Culture* that strangely first reported their initial flight in a cow pasture in Ohio. We spent thirty minutes there, as if it were a chapel, until Pete pulled me to the gift shop full of Wright Brothers memorabilia. I bought him a little snow-dome of Kitty Hawk, with a tiny glider, and two miniature brothers standing proudly by its side. They'd even painted a sliver of a mustache on Orville.

Thomas and Maureen continued to look at the exhibits, but I had to get out to the dusty runway and my boys. Pete ran back into the museum to be with Thomas, as I hurried outside. I took tiny steps on the dirt runway, hoping some part of me would touch the same earth where those brothers had walked.

There was a replica of their little camp building, where the boys lived those exciting days. It was meticulously stocked with jars of food, and had the little desk where they recorded their attempts in the air, as well as their battles with mosquitoes and storms, like grown-up children, playing house.

Ten minutes later, Pete joined me, careening down the runway with his arms outstretched. Thomas came chasing after him. A moment later, Maureen walked out sullenly, squinting into the sun.

"C'mon," I called to her, and we walked the length of the short runway, then up the small hill where the brothers had taken off. There was a soft wind, a good day for flying.

We sat down on the scrubby ground, watching Thomas and Pete play tag.

Maureen was silent and finally I offered, "I'll help with the baby."

"Thanks," she said quietly.

"You know," I said. "When I was fifteen, I had a friend in town, Mary Sorelli, who everybody teased, worse than teased. They used to pull her hair and more. The boys did more. I never spoke up for her, never a word, and then she moved away."

"You should have," said Maureen, "the poor kid."

Pete came panting up the hill. "Do they have jails here? What happens if bad guys bomb the ground where Daddy is, will he get dead again?"

Monday morning, Thomas should have been working up at the Hill, Pete of course should have been in kindergarten, and I should have been listening to the life stories of my students at the YMCA. It was not clear where Maureen should have been, but none of us were in our designated positions. We were having a breakfast picnic of cheese sandwiches and fruit on the beach behind the motel. Pete was digging with his garden shovel, and covering Maureen's feet with sand.

"Were the Wright kids living when there were dinosaurs?" said Pete.

"When there were damn dinosaurs, there were no people. I'm not going to tell you again," said Maureen.

Thomas stood up and stretched. "Anybody for a dip?"

"What's dip?" said Pete.

"You're crazy," I said, as Thomas pulled off his shirt and pants and stood there in the wind in his underwear.

"You're going to get arrested!" warned Pete. "What's dip?"

"C'mon," said Thomas, pulling me to my feet. He started running with me to the water.

Maureen jumped up and stripped off her clothes until she was just wearing a tiny bra and bikini underwear.

"What are they doing?" said Pete.

"C'mon," said Maureen, pulling up Pete. "Let's go swimming."

Thomas and I stopped at the shore, and I said, "Okay, okay," as I yanked off my T-shirt. When I took off my jeans Pete started jumping up and down laughing. Then he pulled off his clothes and threw them in a heap on the sand.

Pete ran to Thomas and put his arms up in the air, and Thomas hoisted Pete onto his shoulders. "We're going to do this!" Thomas screamed. "On your mark, get set, go!" but nobody made a move.

Then Pete yelled, "On your mark, get set, go!" and we all ran into the Atlantic Ocean.

The water was bracing and I got my first mouthful of saltwater. We were all jumping up and down to keep warm. I'd swum hundreds of miles inside at the chlorinated YMCA pool, but I'd never been in an ocean. I swam, slapping the water, fighting, fighting with everything, wanting everything to be regular again.

Finally I was exhausted, and I lay on my stomach with my arms outstretched, just floating along, trying to imagine Wilbur and Orville, in their old-fashioned bathing suits, floating peacefully by my side, but they weren't there. I couldn't feel them the way I used to. I had bigger pictures in my head, stronger images, like slides in a giant slide show, of the rock through Mazur's window, and the Hill House burning down, and the note in my mailbox.

Thomas came over to me and tapped me on my back. I stood up and saw Pete bouncing merrily on his shoulders. Maureen was struggling to get to shore, and I was able to get to her and take her by the hand. We all waded back onto the beach, then threw ourselves down on the sand, panting and surprised like we'd just evolved from the sea. I lay there, with my salty tears dripping into the ground where dinosaurs once walked.

"I'm freezing!" yelled Pete.

"You're not the only one," said Maureen, grabbing her clothes. "I'm going to take a shower."

"I want to go home! Those Wright kids got to go

back to Ohio," said Pete. "I'm going to have a bike store but I won't sell training wheels."

"We have to go home to do that," said Thomas.

At that moment I missed Betty, my eighty-six-year-old student, who read to the class about being a Doughnut Girl in World War II. She wore a uniform and lipstick and drove a special army van in North Africa, where she handed out doughnuts and coffee to our boys, when they returned from bombing raids.

"We should go home," I said quietly, standing up.

"That's the best idea in the tired universe!" said Pete.

"The entire universe," I whispered.

"No, the tired universe," insisted Pete, as the four of us raced back to the motel.

ACKNOWLEDGMENTS

With great thanks to Malaga Baldi, who gives balance and laughter; to Diane Reverand, wise shaper of stories; to Melissa Contreras, who keeps it all together; to Charles Salzberg, baseball consultant; to my students; and to Jake.

READING GROUP GUIDE

1. Hanna's husband died at home. Do you think, if one has the choice, a parent should die at home, or is it too difficult for a child to handle? How do you think it affected Pete?

2. At the start of the book Hanna throws away her husband's slippers. Why do you think she did this?

3. Hanna sleeps with Thomas soon after her husband dies. Do you think she is being disloyal to her husband?

4. When Hanna hears about the crash on September 11th, she goes swimming. Should she have gone to pick up her son at school?

5. Have you experienced or seen any kind of prejudice in your community as a result of September 11th?

6. Do you think Hanna was generous enough to Maureen? How would you have treated this young girl?

7. What do you think of Thomas's relationship to Pete?

8. Should Hanna have tried to help Mazur more?

9. Who do you think set the fire up at the Hill?

10. Do you think Hanna and Thomas will stay together? Would they ever marry?

11. Do you think Maureen will stay with Hanna or Thomas or both of them once she has the baby?

12. How do you think Hanna has changed by the end of the book?

For more reading group suggestions visit
www.stmartins.com

St. Martin's Griffin